IF WINTER
COMES

OTHER BOOKS BY LYNN HALL

IF WINTER COMES

LYNN HALL

Atheneum Books for Young Readers

Atheneum Books for Young Readers
An imprint of Simon & Schuster
Children's Publishing Division
1230 Avenue of the Americas
New York, New York 10020

Printed in the United States of America

Library of Congress Cataloging-in-Publication Data
Hall, Lynn.   If winter comes.
Summary: As an escalating world crisis makes the
threat of nuclear warfare imminent, teenage Meredith
and her boyfriend Barry draw closer to each other
and to other people important to them during what
could be the last weekend of their lives.
[1. Nuclear warfare—Fiction.   2. Interpersonal
relations—Fiction.   3. Conduct of life—Fiction]
I. Title.
PZ7.H1458If   1986   [Fic]   85-43348
ISBN 0-684-18575-X
7 9 11 13 15 17 19 20 18 16 14 12 10 8

IF WINTER COMES

1

On Friday afternoon, May fifth, Meredith McCoy faced her own death on a classroom television screen.

The President of the United States was speaking, with none of his usual confidence. He began by outlining briefly the events that had created the present crisis: since the Second World War there had been a small U.S. air base on an island near Verdura, a tiny republic off the coast of Colombia. Early that spring Verdura's government had been taken over by communist-backed forces, who now demanded the removal of the U.S. Air Force base. The President of the United States refused.

United Nations negotiators had stepped in, but the talks soon bogged down. Two days ago the Verduran government issued their ultimatum: all U.S. troops out of Verdura by eight o'clock Saturday night or atomic missiles, already aimed at major American cities, would be fired.

The President said, "My fellow Americans, I will not try

to deceive you. We are in a time of crisis, of crisis affecting not only our nation but all of mankind."

Meredith McCoy listened with the silent intensity of her classmates and with her own private terror. For the first time in her life she faced the fact that she might be horribly hurt, killed. Now. In the next few days. It could be starting to happen already, with the words coming at her from the television screen.

Meredith was a sturdy young woman, broad-faced and open, with thick waves of sandy hair tied out of her way with a scarf. Her arms were dusted with fuzz and freckles, her wrist bones angular and prominent.

". . . reassure you, my fellow Americans, that although the present situation is grave, your government will do all within its power to bring us safely through . . ."

Meredith shifted in her table-arm plastic chair and leaned forward to doodle on her notebook cover, hiding behind the curtain of her hair. She didn't want to see the President up there on the screen, nor the eyes of her friends around her, glancing, searching for some way to make a joke of this.

It was not a joke, nor a vague threat in the background of her life; some lunatic could push the wrong button and destroy the planet, the human race. That threat had been part of her life for as long as she could remember, but she hadn't taken it seriously. She hadn't let it cloud her life.

Now, suddenly, it was here. Nuclear rockets aimed at American cities.

An ice-water chill trickled through Meredith as she looked

out the classroom window toward the east. Treetops screened the distant gray bulk of Chicago's skyline, unseen from this twenty-mile span, but still there, so close, so familiar, the mass of the city set crisply against the blue haze of the lake, white highways threading suburbs like beads: Oak Park, Elmhurst, Lombard. Home.

The teacher turned off the television, and in the silence of the room, the principal's voice through the intercom announced, "Due to the Verdura crisis, those of you who wish to leave a half an hour early may do so. Have a good . . ." His voice caught and smothered, and the intercom clicked off.

Meredith glanced at Barry and met his eyes. "Have a good weekend" was what Mr. Orlen always said on Friday afternoons. The thought showed in her eyes and in Barry's; Mr. Orlen was as frightened as they were. He couldn't bring himself to wish them a good weekend because he was afraid of what this weekend was bringing.

The teacher said, "All right, you may go," and the class, silent as they had never been silent before, filed out into the hall. Barry and Meredith went down the stairs together, his hand resting on the back of her neck for contact and support.

He was no taller than Meredith, a narrow boy with sharp features beneath black curls. Dark-rimmed glasses dominated his face and created extra eyebrows and temples with their curved, thick lenses.

They didn't speak to each other although they exchanged "see ya's" with friends on their way to their lockers, then out of the building. On the sidewalk leading to the student park-

3

ing lot they walked close to each other, not touching but in step, heads and eyes down, arms around books. Spring sun touched Meredith's hair through her scarf and warmed her scalp.

A longing thudded against her, a longing for nothing to worry about except what the sun was doing to her freckling skin. She lifted her face and squinted up into the bathing warmth. Tomorrow or the next day it might be gone, shut out by a cloud of lethal fallout, death-bearing ash. Nuclear winter.

Still wordless, they walked across the gravel of the parking lot to Barry's gray Honda Civic, and, pitching their books into the back seat, they got in and sat, holding hands automatically.

"So what do you think?" Meredith said finally.

"I think it stinks. The whole thing just . . . I can't live this way, Mare. I mean, how do they expect people to *live* with this kind of thing hanging over them all the time?"

"Well, it's not really . . ."

"No, I mean it. I wish they'd go ahead and fire the damn rockets and get it over with. Wipe the planet clean and let's start over from scratch. I'm not going to live this way, I don't know about you."

"Well, you'll just have to," she snapped. "Just like the rest of us. You're not the only one who's scared here, you know."

"I know it." He pulled her close and rested his cheek against the top of her head. She could feel his breath in her hair and found it comforting. She pretended that Barry was

4

someone bigger and more powerful than she, someone who could actually protect her from what might be coming. After a few minutes, though, because there was no one to protect her, she began to protect Barry, to give him what she so badly needed herself.

"We're just panicking here," she said in a matter-of-fact tone. "It's not going to happen. This is just another political thing, nothing to do with us. There's always some sort of crisis, you know that. Things get blown up out of all proportion by the news guys. Honey, nobody is crazy enough to actually start a nuclear war. Right?"

He didn't answer.

"Right?"

He pulled away and twisted around to tap a cigarette out of the pack on the dash in front of the steering wheel. Meredith punched the car's lighter and held it up for him.

"You're in more danger from those stupid things than from nuclear war, you know that?" she said.

"Listen, let's talk about something else, okay? What do you want to do tonight, go to a show or what?"

"I don't care. What do you want to do?"

"I don't care."

She forced a small laugh. "It's a little hard to get into the mood for Friday night dates with things . . ."

Her voice drifted into silence.

"Yeah, I know." Barry exhaled smoke. "I'll just come over and we'll decide then, okay?"

"Sure. Want to come now?"

"I better get on home. If I get that book report out of the way this afternoon I'll have the weekend free. If we have a weekend. If we have a school to come back to Monday. Oh God, Mare."

He pulled her close again and she could feel his heartbeat against his ribs, even in his wrists where they pressed against her back. She loosened and softened the grip of her arm around him, aware of his breakability. If the worst happened, he would die before she did. She understood that without knowing how. She stroked his back, would have rocked him if the car seats had allowed.

"It's going to be okay," she murmured. "Don't worry."

He nodded against her head, then pulled himself around into driving position. "I'll run you home, okay?"

"No, I've got Mom's car."

The Civic nosed out into the slow-walking flow of students moving toward their cars, then coasted down the row to a little red station wagon and stopped.

"Later," Meredith said with a quick kiss.

"Later."

After he'd driven away, Meredith remembered her books in the back of Barry's car. Oh well, I can get them tonight, she thought. I don't have all that much to do. Sunday night will be plenty of time.

Her mind veered sharply away from the thought that there might not be a Sunday night. Or that the holocaust might be upon them by then, making homework ludicrous.

6

She stopped at the Hi-Vee for a carton of Pepsi, a box of microwave popcorn, and an armful of the gourmet TV dinners she and her mother had been eating lately because they were so easy and so low-calorie. Wheeling the wire cart through the aisles in search of a need she might have forgotten, she became aware that the other shoppers were unusually quiet. Eye contact and smiles and muttered wry comments on the price of lettuce were missing this afternoon.

As she passed the glass-walled manager's office she could see several employees standing inside, arms folded, watching a small TV screen on which two network newsmen were analyzing the President's speech.

The checkout clerk's smile was stiff. "Thank you, have a nice day," she said automatically as Meredith scooped up her sack and gripped the pop carton, but the words had a dead sound, like a touched bell.

From the grocery store Meredith took long-cuts through quiet back streets where she seldom drove. Most of the trees were leafed out already, their branches meeting over the streets. Tulip trees and flowering crabs were pink-blooming mounds in front yards, and beds of purple alyssum bordered walks. The colors seemed fresh washed and brilliant to Meredith. It was like the first sunshine after a summer storm, but there had been no storm.

Only the threat.

And when had it started? She tried to pinpoint it, but couldn't. Wednesday, Monday, a week ago? It had begun so gradually. Meredith seldom watched the national news, and even more seldom thought about it. She listened to weather reports if she was planning something that required good weather; she listened to the sports when they broadcast important local high school scores. Occasionally she paid attention to accident reports involving teenage drivers, or discussions about lowering the legal drinking age in Illinois.

But what went on in the Pentagon or the Middle East or the Soviet bloc, those events were so remote from her life that they simply didn't register in her mind. It was not until sometime during the middle of this week that she had become aware of the Verdura crisis, and then only because her friends and teachers were talking about it.

Only today, when fear was everywhere around her, did Meredith take that fear into herself and feel its ice in her stomach. Only today, only now as she coasted through the placid streets of Lombard, of her world, did she face the possibility that this world might be ending, and her life along with it.

On an impulse she drove south, past Main Street and across the railroad tracks and into the lilac park. Here she slowed the car and crept along, head leaning toward the open window for the fragrance of the purple-mounded bushes that lined the roadway. Beds of garish red and yellow tulips grew in masses beneath the lilacs. Parking the car, Meredith got out and walked up a graveled path to the iron deer. She hadn't visited him for a long time.

He was smaller than she remembered. Stroking the metal ridges of his coat, running a fingertip over the detail of his eye, she remembered being so small she had to reach far above her head to grip the deer's outslanted ear, to swing up onto his back. Daddy had been there to grasp her waist and help her up, to steady her while she rode the statue grinning and waving at Mommy behind the camera.

Hot tears stung behind her eyelids, across the bridge of her nose. She bent and laid her cheek against the metal face of the dear and cried for the little girl who had been so simply happy then.

Sniffing and smearing the wetness off her cheeks, she turned and started back toward the car. A middle-aged man in a business suit stood in the path watching her. He nodded, unsmiling, as though he understood what she was doing there and was waiting his turn to say good-bye to a part of his childhood, too, against the timelessness of the iron deer.

Meredith drove west, out St. Charles Road to the small, square, brick building that was as familiar to her as home. There were no cars parked in front and only Janice's car in the back. Good. Not busy. She parked and pushed through the front door. Gold letters on the glass said, "McCoy Veterinary Clinic, L.H. McCoy, DVM."

At the reception desk Janice looked up and said, "Hi, Merry. How's it going?" Janice was trim and pleasant, with gray-streaked mannish hair. Her professional cheer was a steel-rimmed habit.

"Mom busy?"

"Not too. Go on back."

Behind the reception room a central hallway divided the building and opened on to rooms on either side, two examining rooms, two wards with cages for the patients, an operating room, a large open treatment area, and a tiny bathroom-darkroom for developing X-rays.

Meredith found her mother in the first ward, laying a groggy, belly-bandaged cat onto the freshly newspapered floor of its cage. Lee McCoy was smaller than Meredith, finer boned and blonder, with her hair in a bun at her neck. A light green, blood-spattered professional jacket covered her clothes.

"Hi, sweetie," she said, glancing over her shoulder at Meredith. "Whew. Four spays in a row since lunch. I'm getting too old for this. Just one more little job here, and we can take off. Did you go to the store?"

She arranged the limp cat so that its head and legs were in a comfortable position, raised an eyelid for a quick check of membrane color, and clicked the cage door shut. To Janice she called, "This cat's coming around just fine, Janice. If they want to take her home tonight they can. Back in ten days for sutures."

"Phone on line one," Janice said. "Mrs. Hayden again. The dog is still itching and she says it's driving her nuts."

Lee muttered, "He's going to go on itching till she quits bathing him every day with laundry detergent. Sweetie, get

10

that black cat out of the last cage, will you? I'll be right back."

Meredith opened the cage and lifted out a mammoth old cat with tattered ears and long yellow teeth showing their tips through his lips. His whiskers were bent, broken off.

"Boy, are you ever an ugly old beast."

The cat twisted slowly in her arms until his massive head was butted into the angle of her neck. A rattling vibration from his throat tingled through Meredith as she carried him out to the treatment room table. Automatically she stroked him, raising his hair with static electricity and causing him to arch his back into her palm.

Lee hung up the wall phone and turned to Meredith and the cat. "Well, let's get this over with. I've been putting it off all day.

"Why? What do you have to do to him?"

Her mother gave her a level look.

"Aw, no, Mom, you're not going to put him down, are you? He's purring."

"I can't help that. His owner is tired of spending money on him, says, 'Put him down,' so that's what I've got to do."

"But he's purring. He doesn't want to die."

Their eyes met, mother and daughter, across the cat.

Meredith thought, I don't want to die. I might have to. But he doesn't have to, at least not right this minute. We've got a choice, with him.

Lee reached for the cat, but Meredith took a step backward and wrapped her arms more firmly around the cat. He butted his head against the underside of her chin and purred louder.

"What is it, sweetie? You've seen me put pets down before. You always understood. Didn't you?"

"It's different now," Meredith whispered.

For a moment Lee hesitated, puzzled, studying her daughter's face. "Why different now?"

Meredith shrugged. She didn't understand her feelings clearly enough to put them into words.

"What," Lee said, "because of this Verdura thing, you mean?"

"Maybe. I guess so. I don't know, Mom. I just, I guess I feel like, I don't know, like we shouldn't be wasting any kind of life right now."

Lee sighed and moved to Meredith's side for a shoulder-hug, and rested her head briefly against her daughter's. Then she scratched the cat under one tattered ear and said, "Oh well, I guess we could take him home with us for the weekend, anyway. Then we'll see. Let's get out of here before somebody comes in. Janice, we're off. See you in the morning."

In the storeroom at the back of the building they picked up cat food and litter, then went out the back door to the station wagon.

"You can drive." Meredith relinquished the car keys voluntarily for the first time since she'd had her driver's license. On the six-block drive home, through thickening commuter traffic, she kept her eyes down on the scarred head of the cat in her arms. She felt a need to focus on this one life that she had saved, in order not to have to look out at the blue sky, the budding trees, and the flower-lined walks of the world she had no power to protect.

2

Barry Franklin drove straight home from school. Home was a large dark brick and timbered Tudor with vines on the south wall and a tennis court behind a quadruple garage. An old truck labeled "Han The Lawn Doctor" was parked at the edge of the drive, a mower ramp extending from the rear. Mower and Han were making slow circles of the forested front lawn, perfuming the air with the damp green scent of cut grass and with gas fumes.

Barry waited until Han was looking in his direction, then waved a greeting to the tiny Korean patriarch. Han waved back without seeming to look up from his line of travel. Barry envied Han his tunnel vision. The man seemed to know nothing, care nothing, about anything beyond the immediate job at hand, mulching oak leaves or shaping the hedges at the house's foundation or, today, mowing the lawns. If Barry were to go over there, halt the mower, and ask Han's opinion on the Verdura crisis, probably the old man would say, "Got nothing to do with me." And he would go on mowing.

He's in as much danger as the rest of us, Barry thought, but he's not going through the hell of waiting.

He shook his head and went inside.

Upstairs and to the left of the broad central hall was Barry's room, his suite. The bedroom was spacious, with angled ceilings and dormer window seats. There was a walk-through dressing room with a private bath beyond it, and a tiny kitchenette in one corner, hotplate and microwave and a small refrigerator for soft drinks and the cheese he liked at bedtime. The kitchen had been his birthday present three years ago, along with the redecorating of the entire suite in masculine shades of brown and tan. A kingsized bed replaced the youth bed, and an Apple computer filled the corner where the toy cabinet had been.

Instant manhood at thirteen.

He hadn't been ready for it. He wasn't ready for it now at sixteen.

Sighing, he went to the desk in the study alcove and slouched into the chair. Thousand-word book report. He flipped through his spiral notebook to his jotted notes on *A Farewell to Arms*, then slumped over his typewriter, fighting the knot of tension that, as always, blocked the beginnings of a piece of work. It was easy enough to shut his mind away from thoughts of nuclear attack; he wanted to avoid that. But then came the small panic of blank paper in the typewriter and no words. Even after years of good grades on book reports and themes, Barry always suffered through a sickening certainty that this time his brain would fail him.

Gradually the feeling passed. The first sentence came, and the rest followed, gathering speed as the paragraphs built, and an hour later the report was finished, and it was good.

When am I ever going to start trusting myself? he wondered. He untied his shoes, removed his glasses, and flopped down on the bed. With the typewriter silent he could hear his mother humming in her room across the hall. Her humming made Barry's jaw clench.

What he wanted right now was to be over at Meredith's, in touch with Meredith's courage and energy. He was afraid.

And secretly jubilant. And the fear was as much from the recognition of his joy as it was from the danger that was close around him. Nuclear warheads aimed at him.

It was coming now, this worst of all possible futures that had been in the background of his life always. It was here. Today, tomorrow, Sunday. The hand could push the button. The blinding flash could rip his world apart; the agonizing death could be coming, this Monday, Tuesday. Where would it catch him? In this room? Out on the street somewhere, maybe driving out St. Charles Road toward Meredith's house, maybe on his way to school Monday morning. Maybe tomorrow during the tennis lesson.

Part of his mind was terrified; the other part wanted it to come, longed for the drama, the adrenaline-pumping wild excitement of the end of the world. He wanted to be in on it, wanted to witness it and share in the biggest event in the history of the human race.

But—his thoughts stumbled here—but he didn't want to go through it, not through the actual pain and suffering part of it. He wanted to watch from . . . where? From someplace safe. From beyond his death. Yes. That would be ideal. Get separated from his physical body so there could be no pain, and then watch the spectacle.

Watch it with Meredith, though. He wouldn't want her to suffer, and he knew she was the type who would cling to life even if she was starving, rotting. . . .

His stomach surged and he wondered if he was going to throw up. No, it settled down again. Just stay away from thoughts of rotting. He reached over his head to the headboard bookshelf and got his battered paperback copy of *Life after Life*. For reassurance he leafed through it once again, reading the first-person accounts of the near-death experience as told by survivors of accidents and surgery.

It all sounded so wonderful, the ringing sounds in the head, the floating sensation, and then looking down at your body from above it, hearing people say, "He's dead." And then the floating through the long dark tunnel with the light at the end, the outstretched helping hands of long-dead friends and relatives.

That part worried him. He had no dead friends or relatives; one grandfather who died before he was born, that was all. But he felt confident that there would be a welcoming committee for him anyhow. What came after that was still a mystery because no one who went beyond that point in the drama ever came back to tell about it, but it would be wonderful, he was sure.

It had to be better than this.

He heard himself thinking that, and sneered. Franklin, what have you got to gripe about, you selfish bastard? Here you've got a life thousands of kids would kill for: beautiful home, parents still married to each other, a great girl friend, your own car. This super bedroom. How come none of it seems to be enough?

He knew the answer to that, but he didn't like to look at it. It was all the things he was afraid of. His whole future seemed a mine field waiting to blow him up. All the things that he was supposed to be looking forward to seemed to threaten him. Even sex. He knew that was coming, it was inevitable. Meredith was ready. They'd come close a time or two. But he panicked at the prospect of doing it wrong or awkwardly or foolishly so that all of her life Meredith would remember that her first experience had been with stupid Barry. She might even laugh about it later on, with her other, better lovers.

And there were all those years of college and law school to be survived somehow, all those years of panic attacks before every test, every term paper. Courses ten times harder than high school stuff but still the need to be at the top of every class.

Beyond that, if he survived college and law school, stretched a lifetime of being in practice with his father, with

18

clients who demanded tax loopholes and then bet their futures on the Franklin firm's ability to keep them out of trouble with the IRS. Barry knew himself to be, simply, not up to it.

But he was their only child, only son, only chance for immortality. He'd been hearing that all his life. He had no choice but to be what they needed him to be. No choice except one.

He lifted his head and looked toward the dressing room. He could see himself again as a small child, standing beneath the clothes rod with his bathrobe sash knotted around his neck. He looked up at that rod and rehearsed every move: stand up on the toy chest, tie the sash around the rod, jump off. Be dead, be hanging there when she came up to call him to supper, and she would gather him into her arms and hold him and cry, and feel terrible because she hadn't given him . . .

What was it?

He smiled crookedly. He could remember everything about his first suicide attempt except the reason. Oh, yes. A dog. He'd asked for a dog for Christmas and they'd told him no, a puppy would be too much trouble.

But he hadn't thrown the sash over the rod. He'd stood on the toy chest and stared up at that rod, but after a while he'd climbed down again. And on Christmas morning there was Mugwump tied to the banister, wagging his beagle tail and scratching the woodwork. Mugwump had spent four months making irreparable stains on the wool carpet and claw marks on the doors, and had finally run away, to everyone's relief.

But the memory of that gift stayed with Barry. It was proof of his power. He had only thought of killing himself and presto, he got his puppy.

Even when he grew old enough to realize that there was no real connection between his desire to kill himself and the buying of the puppy, the essence of the idea remained in his mind. It was the only kind of power he had ever known, over his parents, over his life. It was the only *choice*.

As he lay there in the middle of his bed it occurred to him that a decision had been made on some unconscious level of his mind. If the holocaust came, if the worst happened, he would engineer his own exit. There would be no suffering through a nuclear winter for him.

Through the open window he could hear his father talking to Han, helping him get the mower up its ramp into the truck, paying him for today's mowing, and saying he'd better come again around Tuesday or Wednesday, at the rate the grass grows this time of year.

Barry got up, retied his shoes, and went downstairs. His father was just coming in the front door. Joel Franklin was slight, like his son, with close-cropped wiry black hair, neither graying nor receding. It wouldn't dare, Barry had sometimes thought, for in spite of the man's small stature, Joel Franklin radiated force. He charged the air with it when he entered a room. His movements were quick and sure and never undirected. Even when he paced, which he did frequently, he gave the impression of traveling somewhere specific.

Joel deposited his alligator attache case in its corner of the

20

entrance hall and looked up toward Barry on the stairs. "You been listening to the news?"

Barry leaned against the newel post and ran his thumbnail around its carving. "Not since school. We watched the President's press conference in class, and then they let school out a half hour early. It must be serious, to let school out early, huh?"

He followed his father through the soft green expanse of living room, into the creams and golds of the formal dining room beyond, to the antique walnut bar in the corner near the French doors to the patio. Joel poured himself a tumbler of Chivas Regal usually reserved for impressing company. Abruptly he turned and looked at his son.

"Want a drink?"

Startled, Barry shook his head. That offer had never been made before.

"Where's your mother?" Joel said.

A feminine voice behind them said, "Kitchen."

"She sounds cheerful," Joel muttered.

"She's always cheerful." Barry and his father exchanged quick, loaded looks, then moved together through the French doors and onto the stone-flagged patio beyond. The view was restricted by high shrubbery at their property boundary, but all within that boundary was as perfect as Han could make it: smooth expanses of lawn swirling around gracefully curved flower beds and flagstone walks, a terraced descent to the lower lawn where the chain link fence around the tennis court was camouflaged with greenery. It was a lawn

21

intended for entertaining. At the edge of the patio stood an oversized charcoal broiler big enough to cook steaks for the neighborhood. The filigreed white iron lawn furniture was luxuriously padded so that guests could sit comfortably on elegance.

Joel and Barry stood at the edge of the patio, each leaning on a separate pillar, each staring out at nothing. Barry wanted to stand closer to his father, but there seemed no way to get there.

"You think it's serious?" he asked finally.

Joel looked at him. "The news, you mean?"

Barry nodded.

"Oh yes. Serious. Sure."

"Do you think it's going to, you know, happen?"

Joel seemed not to move, but his drink sloshed over the rim of his glass and trickled down over his fingers.

"It could. It could happen."

"What'll we do if it does? I mean, do you have any plan or anything like that?"

"Plan? No. No plan. Nothing we can do. No point in hiding in cellars, as though it was a tornado and everything will be all right as soon as it blows over. If those lunatics start a nuclear war, it's not ever going to be all right again, not for anybody. So don't expect me to do anything about it," he shouted.

Barry shrank from his father's anger. "Don't yell at me about it. It's not my fault."

Joel looked away, across the lawn. There were white lines

around his mouth and at the sides of his nose, and a staring immobility of his eyes that Barry had never seen before.

"Dad?"

"Hm."

"Are you scared?"

"Everybody with a mind is scared, Barry."

In the stillness they both were aware of humming from the kitchen.

Barry left his pillar and moved closer to his father, within arm's reach. But Joel didn't reach. He tilted up his glass and went on staring at the deepening blue of the evening sky.

Just over the tops of the boundary trees the first few stars brightened, one larger than the others. Silently Barry said, "Star light, star bright, very first star I see tonight, I wish I may, I wish I might, have the wish I wish tonight."

He closed his eyes and thought, I don't know what I wish. That it was all over, one way or another. Either that it doesn't happen or else that I get through it somehow without being more scared or more hurt than I can stand.

Dinner was served not in the formal dining room but at the round oak table at the far end of the oversized kitchen. Meatloaf and au gratin potatoes and green beans with slivered almonds, a huge salad but no dessert. It was the kind of dinner a model housewife would serve to a family whose health she cared about. Beverly Franklin had read all the right magazines and formed her habits before her life had begun slowing and blurring.

She was taller and heavier than Barry or Joel, a soft blond

23

woman whose early beauty had not left her, only become less clearly defined as she aged. She seldom wore makeup, seldom got fully dressed unless she was leaving the house, and she did that less and less often now, and never alone. Barry or Joel drove her to the grocery store or the shopping mall, or did her errands for her after school or after work. Although she was never dirty nor uncombed, it was not unusual for her to go all day in the same dressing gown.

As Barry and Joel pulled out their chairs and settled at the table Beverly said, "Well, what kind of day did you have, Joel? Barry? Anything exciting?"

Barry stared at his mother.

Joel said, "You've been listening to the news, haven't you, Bev?"

She smiled and passed the beans. "Not really. All they talked about on the 'Today Show' this morning was all that war business in Venezuela or wherever. It was depressing. I just turned it off and listened to music. I got out that old Gilbert and Sullivan album, you remember that one?" She began to sing.

"Mom," Barry said, holding the bean dish, "how can you think about music now? Haven't you been following what's going on out there?"

"Never mind, son," Joel said sharply.

Beverly looked from Barry to Joel, a softly puzzled expression on her face, as though she was trying to figure out how she had angered them.

24

Joel said, "The Tax Attorneys' Association luncheon was today, hon. You'd have loved the restaurant. It was in Old Town, one of those remodeled warehouse places, and the food was really something. I had scampi, and it was darn near as good as we had that time in New Orleans, remember? You'd like this place. We'll go there for dinner next time we're in town for the evening, okay?"

Barry watched the two of them, watched his father slipping into his mother's game. He wanted to yell at them. He wanted them to be as churned up inside as he was, and instead they were swallowing meatloaf and potatoes and talking about eating dinner in town one of these nights, just as though there was no question that there would be a future of evenings in town.

Barry looked at the food on his plate and his stomach clenched shut. He got up.

Beverly turned her smiling face toward him and said, "Where are you off to tonight? Going out with Meredith?"

"Yeah."

"Bring her back here if you feel like it. Martins are coming over later on."

"I don't know what we're going to do."

"Well, have a nice evening."

Barry stared at her. Have a nice evening? He looked at his father and caught the full force of Joel's eyes. They said, *Leave her alone. One of us might as well be happy.*

Barry shrugged and left.

3

The Algonquin Apartments were a trio of dark brick buildings set in a U-shape around a timber-terraced parking area. Boston ivy covered the bottom third of the buildings, and large oaks gave an appearance of shade and weathered solidity. The rule was no pets except caged birds, but any resident whose cat or small dog did not call attention to itself was allowed to keep the animal so long as the building manager was not forced to admit that he knew about it. Cats who were just visiting for the weekend posed no problem.

On the middle floor of the middle building the McCoys' two-bedroom extra-large looked out over tennis courts and pool. "Extra-large" referred to the fact that the living room stretched the full depth of the apartment, and there were two full baths and a genuinely comfortable dining area at the end of the kitchen. The deck overlooking the back lawn was double width, too, and there was a working gas fireplace in the long wall of the living room.

Although the decor was standard apartment colors, white walls and green carpets, the place was a definite step up from their previous apartment. Lee and Meredith had moved into the Algonquin two years ago when Lee's practice netted its first forty-thousand-dollar profit year.

Meredith liked the Algonquin. She liked the quality aura of the ivy-covered buildings, the timbered terraces, and the heavy solid feel of the glass doors as she unlocked them. She appreciated the smooth solidity of the oak stair rail and the genuine brass plate that said 6B on her door.

She had vague plans to live here with her mother for a long time, through college anyway. Then maybe she'd have one of the little efficiency apartments downstairs when she started working as a therapist or counselor, whichever it turned out to be. It would be ideal, she'd thought, having her own place but in the same building as her mother so they would always have each other for company if they wanted.

But tonight the Algonquin seemed insufficient shelter. Meredith stood beside her bedroom window staring out at the sunset and thinking, The fallout can come right in around these windows.

With a hard shake of her head she turned and went into the bathroom and began to fill the tub. Friday night date. No real reason not to follow the familiar pattern, not yet. She shaved her legs, nicking her kneecap in the usual place. With unseeing automation she lotioned her elbows and powdered her stomach and back and shoulders, then let the water out of the tub and wandered back into her room.

27

Wear. Wear. What to wear. Didn't matter. Probably wouldn't go anywhere anyhow. She stood staring at her closetful of clothes.

From the doorway Lee said, "Why don't you wear that new Calvin Klein dress? That looked so cute on you."

"I was going to save it for special," Meredith said, but she reached for it anyway. It was a heavy denim shirtwaist dress, loose and full and surprisingly soft against her skin. Might as well wear it, she thought. There might not be a . . . better time.

"It looks great," Lee said. "I can't wait to borrow it." She wore faded jeans and a huge wine-red sweater, and her hair straggled casually away from its knot. The cat came padding and mrowring down the hall to rub against Lee's leg. She picked him up.

The buzzer rang. Barry. Meredith buzzed him in and opened the apartment door. "Hi."

"Hi. Here's your books, you left them in the car. Hi, Lee. Where'd the cat come from?"

Before Lee could answer, Meredith saw "Special Bulletin" flash on the television screen in the far corner of the room.

"Something's happening," she said. They turned up the volume and sat together on the sofa, Meredith in the middle.

The CBS anchorman greeted them and said in a crisp voice that the President would be addressing them shortly from the Oval Office.

Meredith sat forward, and Lee and Barry with her. She

28

realized they were holding hands, all of their hands clustered on her knees.

"My fellow Americans," the President said, "I had hoped by this time to be able to tell you the crisis had passed. Unfortunately, this is not the case. In spite of continued efforts by UN negotiators, the situation remains stalemated. Governor Cassals of Verdura has once again repeated his threat to bomb American cities if U.S. Air Force personnel is not removed from Verdura by eight o'clock eastern time, tomorrow evening."

Meredith felt her face go stiff and pale. She felt catapulted toward disaster. Her fingers squeezed tightly around her mother's and Barry's.

The President was saying, ". . . We must stand tough. We must hold to the belief that sanity and self-preservation will stop the Cassals government short of the ultimate idiocy, the firing of nuclear weapons. I will be holding press conferences as often as is necessary over the next twenty-four hours, so that you will have news of developments as soon as they reach the White House."

Lee snorted. "I wish he'd spend less time calling press conferences and more time getting us out of this mess. What do your folks think of it?" She leaned around Meredith to look at Barry.

He shrugged. "Dad's scared stiff but won't talk about it. My mom's just . . . her usual self."

"Spaced out?" Meredith said.

He nodded. "Off in her own little time warp. Tonight at supper she was singing Gilbert and Sullivan music."

"Well," Lee said, "we all handle crises in different ways, I guess."

"I don't think she even knows there is a crisis. It's getting so she's this way all the way. Hell, she's getting prescription tranquilizers from four doctors that I know of. Maybe more. I can't remember when I've seen her actually in focus."

Meredith said, "Why doesn't your dad do something, Barry? He must know what's going on, doesn't he?"

"Oh, sure. I don't think he realizes how bad it is, but he's got to know she's not right. I don't know. What could he do?"

The three sat silently. On the television screen the President left the podium and an announcer said, "Our regularly scheduled programs will not be seen tonight. Instead we will be bringing you a CBS special, 'Deadly Winter,' next. 'Dallas' and 'Falcon Crest' will return next week at their regularly scheduled times."

The documentary began with a panel discussion of the probable effects of nuclear war on the planet Earth. Panelists included a nuclear physicist, a noted biologist, an anthropologist from Duke University, and a best-selling author of science fiction.

"I'm not sure I want to watch this," Meredith said in a small voice. The others muttered agreement, but no one got up to change the channel.

One after another the four panelists added their individual

expertise to the scenario: the square-mile radius from the bomb's target in which all life would be killed instantly; the wider radius in which nonsheltered life would die within days of radiation burns and sheltered life would survive slightly longer, to die of internal radiation poisoning from contaminated food, water, and air.

Then, beyond the immediately affected area, and gradually spreading to cover the entire planet, would come the nuclear winter, the sun's disappearance behind all-encompassing clouds of nuclear ash. Fallout from the ash would destroy crops and livestock so that there would be no food this year, next year. The soil would be too contaminated to grow new crops even if clean seed existed, and it wouldn't. The food chain of interdependent plants and animals would be broken beyond repair, at least for many years to come.

With the sun hidden, the earth's temperature would drop so low that only one form of earthly life could survive the nuclear winter. Insects.

The meek would inherit the earth.

"But that can't happen," Meredith whispered. "That's just too . . ."

"Bizarre," Lee said in a tightened voice.

Barry said nothing.

The cat came unnoticed and stretched himself out across their laps, purring.

As the program progressed, showing film clips from science fiction movies, the three on the sofa moved closer together until they were joined in a three-way hug, arms tight around each other, holding on for dear life.

Meredith curled against Barry's ribs and stared out the car window at the apartment buildings around them, the other cars in the lot, the oak tree whose branches screened the bright slice of new moon.

It's safe for now, she thought. Tonight we have it. We can see the moon and all those gorgeous stars. It won't be till tomorrow night. . . .

All of her senses were expanding; she heard night insects in the trees and semis on the expressway and rock music from somewhere, and Barry's breath in her hair and his heart under her left ear. She saw the washed green of the grass under the light pole, the diamond gleam of light on a car's chrome strip, individual threads in Barry's shirt and the pores of his skin on the inside of his wrist. She smelled damp grass and tasted a bit of meat rotting between her molars.

She felt a tingling through her body, everywhere, fingertips to the soles of her feet. Even her hair felt alive.

She wanted to make love. For the first time in her life she actively wanted to conceive a new life. It was a powerful feeling that, oddly, had no real connection with Barry, only with herself and the womb within her and the universe beyond the car window.

And the nuclear winter that had the power to end the human race.

Every atom in Meredith McCoy raged to fight back.

"You're sure quiet," she said, squeezing Barry lightly.

"This is not exactly a joyous occasion, you know."

"What are you thinking?"

He shrugged. "Oh, just about tomorrow night, the whole thing. You know. How to get through it if it happens."

She lifted her head and looked at him. "What's there to think about? If it happens it happens. I don't see that we have much choice about how to get through it. Do you?"

"We have a choice. I know one thing for sure, I'm not going to die a lingering death. If it happens, and if I survive the . . . initial blast like they were talking about on television, I'm going to make darn sure I get out of it before the poisoning and starvation part come. Aren't you?"

"You mean suicide?" she whispered.

"Sure. It's the only sensible thing. And I want us to do it together."

"Barry!" She sat away from him, curled up against the far door, and stared at his profile.

They sat without speaking for several minutes while he lit a cigarette, then held it, watching the glowing tip but not smoking it.

"You want to know what I was thinking?" Meredith said finally. "I was having this really strong urge to get pregnant."

He stared at her. "You've got to be out of your gourd. How could anybody want to start a baby at a time like this?"

Meredith shrugged. "I didn't say it was logical, I just said that was what I was feeling."

He threw the cigarette out his window and the glowing

tip made a beautiful rainbow arc against the blackness. An ache overwhelmed Meredith and she began to cry, softly at first and then with mounting despair. She covered her face with her hands and needed Barry to pull her close.

He only gripped her knee and said, "What brought that on?"

She shook her head. "I saw a rainbow the other day. Sunday. Remember how it rained in the afternoon and then it cleared in the west but there were still those big purply clouds to the east? And there was this huge double rainbow, a big one with a little one inside it. It only lasted about five minutes. I watched the whole thing. It was so beautiful, Barry."

"Aw, come on, Mare. Honey. Don't cry. I know how you feel, but . . ."

"No, you don't," she flared, stiffening. "I don't think you ever looked at a rainbow in your life, Barry. At least not the way . . . you don't, you know, *love* things like I do."

"I love you."

That stilled her, but only for a moment. In a low voice she said, "You couldn't really love me. I think you're too scared to love anybody or anything. You're always talking about killing yourself, or . . ."

"I'm not either. Don't be stupid."

"Well, you think about it. You know you do. You tried it that time when you were little. You told me about that several times, so it must be in your mind. And now, now

34

with this"—she motioned vaguely toward the world outside the car—"when all of a sudden we could really *lose* everything, what's the first thing you think about? Suicide. You should be hanging on to every second of life we've got, while we've got it."

"Like you."

"Yes, like me. What's wrong with that?"

"Nothing. But I'm not you."

"No, you sure as heck are not me. You want to know something else I think?"

He sat back from her and sighed.

"You want to know what else I think?" she insisted. "I think you about half want that bomb to drop. I think you want somebody else to do it for you. It's some kind of easy way out or something. And I have *never*"—she pounded his leg with her fist—"I have never understood what it is about your life that you hate so much that you'd even consider ending it. You have so much!"

He was silent. He turned his head away from her and stared out into the night.

"Talk to me, Barry. Tell me."

He shrugged.

"Are you scared?" she probed.

"I don't know. Maybe. I guess."

"What of?"

He shrugged again. "Lots of things. Dentists."

Meredith smiled, grinned, chuckled. "You want the world

35

to blow up so you won't have to go to the dentist anymore? That really makes sense."

His face twisted against the pull of a smile. He drew her close and they held each other for a long quiet time. Finally he said, "One thing you're more afraid of than I am is saying you love me. I know you feel it, Mare, but you never say it."

It was true, Meredith recognized that. One of the best things about Barry was that the attraction had always been equal between them. Unlike Scott. With Scott she had always been the wanter; wanting him to notice her, to call her, to spend time with her. And when he did those things it was always with an air of conferring a favor upon her. She was forever grateful and it soured her toward him in the end.

Then Barry Franklin began to emerge from a familiar face to an entity with a name and home and family behind him. He began going through classroom doors with her, exchanging greetings, then comments and jokes, and finally real conversations. Rides home from school expanded into dates, then into a going-together relationship, and through it all the balance had been equal. The wanting was equal, so that neither was begging, neither was conferring favors.

It was only in saying "I love you" that a division was showing up. At first Meredith accepted the words from Barry with a kind of wonder, underlaid by uneasiness. Even though it felt good, wonderful, to be told she was loved, it called for an answer and she couldn't give it. Barry said, "I love you," and waited, and needed to hear it back, and she couldn't.

She was afraid. She was afraid of him in some way, afraid to increase his feelings for her.

He murmured, "You won't tell me you love me but yet you sit here talking about wanting to get pregnant. That doesn't make any sense."

"Oh Barry." She sat up away from him again and reached for the car door. "How can you expect me to make any sense at a time like this? And I wish you'd quit pushing me. You know and I know that I feel as much for you as you do for me. I'm not ready for anything . . . I can't . . . don't push me, okay?"

He raised his hands in the air.

She got out of the car and stood in front of the open door, hesitant to leave him with roughened emotions between them but needing to get away from him. "What are you going to do tomorrow?"

"I don't know. What are you?"

"I don't know. Maybe go out and see my dad or something."

"Well, maybe I'll see you. Tomorrow night anyway, okay?"

She nodded, slammed the door, stood on the walk while his car backed out and disappeared down the road. Tomorrow night. Cold dread settled in her stomach again. As she walked toward the door she became aware of the rasping song of night insects in the trees. Insects. She shuddered and hurried inside.

The apartment was dark, her mother already in bed. Meredith tiptoed through to her own room and got into her nightshirt, but there was still a need in her that kept her from lying down in her own bed. She padded to the door across the hall and stood there, looking in.

"I'm awake," Lee said.

"Want company?"

"Sure."

The cover was lifted and Meredith crawled gratefully in. They lay side by side, not touching but aware of each other's warmth.

"Mom?"

"Mm."

"I just had the funniest feeling, sitting out there in Barry's car."

"What was that?"

"I had this huge urge to, you know, make love. Isn't that weird? I mean, I've never felt anything like that before. I mean, a little bit sometimes when Barry and I would be messing around, you know. But then it was more really just, I don't know, responding to him, I guess. Him getting turned on would kind of turn me on a little bit, but it was more mental than physical, if you know what I mean."

"I do."

"Well, but tonight was different. It was so . . . *strong*, Mom. It really shook me."

"The question is, did it shake him?" Lee asked dryly.

"Oh, he didn't know about it. I mean, I told him, kind of, more or less. But he was way off in another direction. You know what he was thinking about, at that same time? Suicide."

"Seriously, do you think?"

"Who knows, with him. Maybe. I mean, if this thing happens. I wouldn't put it past him. Did I tell you about that time when he was a little kid, when he almost hanged himself over some Christmas present he didn't think he was going to get? Did I tell you about that?"

"Yes. And I told you I didn't like the idea of your dating someone that unstable, remember?"

"Yeah, but then we got to know him better and he seemed okay. I mean, a little kid can do weird things sometimes. And he didn't actually do it, only planned it. But I do think he'd be the type that wouldn't want to try to survive a nuclear winter. Don't you?"

Lee rolled over on her side, facing Meredith. The cat at the foot of the bed complained and readjusted his position against her legs.

"I expect if worst came to worst, there'd be a whole lot of people who would choose a quick death over a slow lingering one," she said.

Meredith lay on her back, hands behind her head. "I

know, and it probably makes sense, and maybe I'd even want to go that route myself, I'm not sure. But yet here I am with this huge urge to, I suppose, get pregnant. That makes no sense at all."

"Oh, it does in a way." Lee reached out and stroked her daughter's arm. "I've read where lots of people have an overwhelming sexual urge at the time of the death of a parent or spouse. Nobody ever used to admit it, because it seemed so shameful, but now they're finding out that it's a common phenomenon. Probably nature's way of keeping the species going. Strong life force in the face of death, you know. Renewing ourselves."

They were silent a long time, then Meredith whispered, "But if the nuclear winter comes, it won't do any good, will it? All those natural urges won't have a chance."

"No, baby. They won't."

"Are you scared, Mom?"

"Yes."

Several minutes later Meredith said, "Are you still awake?"

"Umhm."

"You know something else? Somtimes I almost wish I was more like Barry. I mean, if . . . worst comes to worst . . . it would be less terrible if you wanted to die already. If you were already more or less suicidal by nature, and weren't afraid of dying, it wouldn't be so . . . unbearable." Her voice cracked. "I don't want to lose anything, Mom. Or anybody."

They nestled together and wept, and Lee stroked her

daughter's shoulder, hair, arm. "You're the lucky one, sweetie, not Barry. You have the capacity to love. That's always more risky than running away from things like Barry does."

"But that's not true, Mom. He tells me he loves me, and I can't say it back to him. I feel terrible about that. I know it's a brave thing, to tell someone you love them, and Barry can do that and I can't. So in that way he's the strong one, between the two of us." She sniffed.

"Maybe you don't want to say it because you don't feel it," Lee said reasonably.

They lay in the silence, with Meredith sniffing occasionally, and someone in the apartment above them walking with heavy pounding steps. "I don't think it's that, exactly. It's more like, I don't know. He scares me in a way. He's so intense. Maybe I feel like if I tell him I love him, and then later on I change my mind or realize I was wrong about it, maybe he'd do something to himself and it would be my fault. I just don't want to be . . . responsible." She shuddered.

The man upstairs thudded back across the ceiling.

"Well, that's understandable," Lee said. "Barry isn't a very strong person for you, for you to lean on, if you know what I mean. Not very stable. You're probably wise not to let him get too dependent on you."

"But I do really mostly love him, more or less. I could open up and tell him so, and sometimes I almost have, and lots of times I really want to, but I just—he—I don't know . . ."

41

"He scares you."

"Yeah."

Lee's voice was rich with smile. "There ain't no easy answers, kid."

Meredith sniffed again. They quit talking then, but they didn't sleep.

4

"I think I'll go out and see Dad today. Would that be okay?"

Meredith ate her toast over the kitchen sink. Her eyes were puffy from lack of sleep, her hair was a wild tangle. Toast crumbs hung on the front of her nightshirt.

"Fine with me," Lee said. "Call and see if he can meet you at the station, and I'll drop you off on my way to work. I'm going to need the car this afternoon for groceries."

Meredith made the call, then hurried to dress and beat her hair down with a brush, as Lee stood at the front door waiting. Jeans, scoop-neck tee shirt, hooded sweatshirt against the morning's chill, denim shoulder bag.

"Ready."

They drove wordlessly to the train station where Chicago-bound shoppers replaced the weekday commuters on the platform. Meredith waved her mother off, then bought her ticket and crossed to the outbound side of the platform to wait for the familiar Aurora train.

When it came she settled in her seat, conscious of possible lasts. Last time to sit on these ribbed gray cushions in a nearly empty coach on a Saturday morning, going out to see Dad. Last time to surrender her ticket to the conductor who swayed down the car like a shoelace, back and forth, missing no seat, no passenger, but never seeing the people, only the tickets.

It was a forty-minute ride to Aurora, the last stop on the commuter line. As Meredith stepped down from the train her father pushed away from the wall he'd been leaning on and came to wrap her in a hug. "How you doing, kiddo?"

Mike McCoy was an angular man, with a long Norwegian face and a halo of frizzy sandy hair that stood out from a hairline halfway back on his skull. The hirsute halo went all the way around his face in a circle of beard several shades redder than the hair. His jeans were torn at the knee and faded almost white, as was the plaid of his flannel shirt. An aroma of pig manure rose from his boots.

"Hi, Pop." Meredith returned his hug and stayed latched to him longer than usual. "Thanks for coming to get me. I just had this sudden urge to see you."

"The pleasure is half mine, I'm sure. Come on, the truck's over here."

They drove for half an hour over ever-diminishing roads, between fields where tractors combed the gray-tan winter earth into moist black spring soil. Farmhouses stood close to the road, sheltered to the north and west by double, triple rows of windbreak pines. Every farmstead showed life; people mowing lawns or conferring under the raised hood of an old car or stretching barbed wire on newly set steel posts.

"It's just like it always is," Meredith wondered aloud.

"You've been watching the news? Is that why the sudden urge to see old Dad?"

"Oh, I always want to see you, you know that." She slapped his leg.

He captured her hand and held it. "I know. I always want to see you, too. We just don't always have the time, or take the time, do we? Not till something like this comes along and shakes us up." He lifted her hand and rubbed his bearded chin against the back of it. "If you hadn't called this morning, I was going to come in to town tonight to see you and your mom."

"That's good. Dad?"

"Yo."

"Is it going to happen?"

"How should I know?"

"But what do you think? Come on, tell me. It's important."

He thought a long time, then said, "I give it a fifty-fifty chance."

"And if they do bomb us, do you think anybody is going to survive?"

Slowly he shook his head. "I don't see how they could. I've thought about it and thought about it, and I just don't see how *Homo sapiens* is going to get himself out of this one, if it goes that far. I don't think the species can survive a nuclear winter, hon."

45

"You say that so calmly."

He shrugged. "Panic is not going to do a hell of a lot of good here, is it?"

"Nothing is," Meredith said bleakly.

"Ah, it hasn't happened yet and maybe won't. We're picking peas today. Want to help? You can shell if you want, a nice sitting-down job."

She pulled in a deep breath and forced her mind into today. This time, this place. Brilliant blue sky arching over the world, little flat-bottomed white clouds far out above the horizon. Rich green of the grass along the roadside.

"Look up there." She pointed to a hawk perched on a power line.

The truck slowed and turned in at the familiar farm lane, a dirt track that led straight as fencing for a quarter of a mile between poplar trees and level fields, to the house and buildings. Meredith had been coming to the farm for seven years now, two or three times a month, since her father came to live there. Twice she spent most of her summer vacation there. It was familiar and comfortable and welcoming, even though the faces sometimes changed.

She had long since gotten over her anger toward the farm and the people on it, for taking her father away from her. Seeing how happy he was here, seeing how happy her mother was with her life in Lombard, Meredith had gradually come to accept that it was necessary for the two of them to live separate lives, at least for now. The love wasn't

46

dead between them; it was at the back of their daily lives somewhere, but it existed.

The farm and its divergent family had grown through the past seven years into a working organism. Chuck Davenport, who had been Mike's department head in the insurance agency where Mike had been an underwriter, inherited the farm from his grandmother. Chuck had spent his childhood on the farm and loved it. It was a good farm, two hundred acres, almost all tillable, some of the richest earth on earth, and mortgage-free.

At first Chuck and his wife lived on the farm and commuted to their jobs, but gradually Chuck's interest centered more and more on the farm. When his wife died of Hodgkin's disease Chuck took early retirement from the company and spent two years living a hermit's existence in the old farmhouse. His only regular visitor was Mike McCoy who, having grown up on a farm in Wisconsin, came to love the place almost as much as Chuck did. The two men began to talk about the possibility of running the farm as a cooperative, if they could find the right people.

The right people proved to be the elusive ingredient in the farm's success. Young people were too rootless, too aimless, and too unwilling to work and to commit themselves. Older people were often inflexible in their habits. They came, they stayed a month or a season or a year, then moved on.

Lee McCoy refused to come at all. She argued hotly and

coldly that she had worked her fanny off putting herself through college and vet school, and had built her practice up from a scary in-debt nothing to a dependably profitable livelihood, and she was damned if she would throw all that away just because he had this wild hare about returning to the land and living in some commune that was doomed to fail because those things always did and if Mike weren't such an adolescent he would know that. She had a child to support and that called for security; she loved him but no way in hell was she going to follow him to that crazy farm.

Mike went anyway. It was on a trial basis at first, a year's leave of absence from the insurance agency, a trial separation from Lee. But it took. He stayed on the farm. The separation was never finalized into divorce, but yearly it grew more real as his life and Lee's developed in opposite directions.

Through a sifting process four more people emerged and stayed: Jean and Robert Ling, Harv and Margaret Epps. Between them and Chuck and Mike, the farm stabilized and began to produce the lifestyle and the comparative security that its people wanted. There was little cash income, but little need for it. Most of the land was rented to neighboring farmers, and the rent paid the taxes and the utility bills. The house was heated by a mammoth wood furnace for which the men cut and hauled wood from the farm's woodlot. Almost all of their food was homegrown.

The main work of the farm was the growing and selling of vegetables, which were picked daily in season and sold at farmers' markets in nearby towns and the outer suburbs. With

no middlemen to cut into the profits, and with superior produce to offer, the farm made more than enough in profit to
pay for the operating expenses and cash needs of its six
people.

The house stood to the right of the lane as they drove in.
It was big and square and unlovely, and dear. Old elms
shaded the yard, where dogs and cats stretched or wandered
in search of a better place to stretch. A roofed breezeway
connected the house with a smaller building that had been
a garage but was now a work area for processing the vegetables. Beyond this building, barn and corncrib and chicken
house and hog house were scattered about a turnaround
circle.

Mike parked the pickup near the house, and Meredith
jumped down. Margaret Epps was seated in the breezeway,
shelling peas into a pan in her lap. Meredith bent for the
woman's hug and cheek-kiss. "Hi, Margaret."

"Hi, love. Mike, they need the pickup out in the field."

As Mike drove off in the direction of the bent figures in the
field beyond the hog house, Meredith pulled up another
lawn chair and found a sack of unshelled peas and a pan to
shell into.

A small television set was perched on a stump, its cord
disappearing through the workshed window. In the sunlight
its picture was invisible, but overlying the farmsong of hens
fussing over discarded pea pods and pigs clanking feeder
covers and a tractor in the distance, Meredith heard the
newsman's voice.

Meredith looked at Margaret and clenched her jaw. The older woman shook her head. "Not getting any better."

She was a blocky woman who seemed designed for a rocking chair. Her jowls were pendulous, her gray hair chopped short, her features severe within their pads of flesh. Around her eyes was a heaviness that had come with the loss of her own farm, six years ago, in an FHA foreclosure. Neither her grandchildren nor her new home here nor a bright and fragrant May morning could completely lift the sadness of that loss. It seemed to Meredith that Margaret Epps had already suffered the ultimate loss; whatever came now would be anticlimactic.

Through the late morning they shelled peas, working without talking for the most part, listening to news broadcasts that only repeated themselves, listening to the rain of peas stripped from their wombs by quick thumbs and aimed into pans. In spite of the newsmen's words Meredith found herself lulled by the rhythm of the work.

It couldn't happen here, she thought, tilting her head back to rest her neck, and seeing a game of squirrel tag in the branches of the elm overhead.

Toward noon the pickup came back with Mike and Jean in the front, Chuck and Harv and several bushels of new-picked peas in the back. Margaret got up and went inside to start lunch.

Jean Ling was Meredith's favorite of the farm people. She was small and childlike in her overalls, her face thin and brown, her dark hair cut short. She could have been any

50

age within ten years in either direction from her actual thirty.

She called, "Meredith. Come over here, I've got something to show you. I'm glad you came out today. Come here, look."

She and Meredith walked across the circle to a rail fence that enclosed an old orchard. The few remaining apple trees were twisted and overgrown and almost ready to blossom.

"You got your lambs," Meredith sang. "Oh, they're adorable."

Five ewes grazed or dozed within the orchard fence, one huge with unborn young, the others with babies asleep beside them or playing in the long grass.

"Seven lambs already," Meredith said, impressed. "And two black ones. Oh, great. Just what you wanted."

Jean climbed the fence and went in among them, and Meredith followed. "Three pairs of twins so far," Jean said, "and I'm sure Crabby Mary is carrying twins, too, she's so huge. I really wasn't expecting the blacks, but I was hoping. Now I'll be able to finish that black coat I was working on. I showed you that, didn't I? I just love that soft charcoally color. And for sweaters, just think. Gorgeous. I think your mom was wanting a sweater if I ever get enough black wool."

Meredith sat in the grass and held her fingers out to the nearest lamb, who approached slowly, curiously. He sniffed her fingertips, wrapped his tongue around them for a quick suck, then, disappointed, bounded away shaking his long tail. A bolder baby came close and stood with one tiny hoof on Meredith's thigh while it ran its muzzle over her ear and into

51

her hair. She giggled and the lamb bounced back a step.

"They've got to be the cutest things in the world," Meredith said. "How can you stand the thought . . ."

"What, that the world is going to go *poof* in the next twenty-four hours? It's not." Her voice was airy, assured.

"How do you know that?" Meredith twisted around to look at her.

"I don't *know* it any more than the croaking ravens *know* that it will happen. I just believe that it won't."

"Because you don't want to believe it could."

"No, because I can't believe God went to all this trouble for nothing."

"Maybe this is like Armageddon or whatever, you know, wiping out mankind and starting over again without the sin, something like that."

Jean shook her head. "I can't buy that. I think people are good, mostly. I know lambs are good, and all the rest of the animals. If God wanted to punish us, I don't think He'd wipe out everything along with us. So it's not going to happen, so quit scaring yourself to death about it, okay?"

Meredith stared at Jean, hoping to find a reason in that face to believe her. She didn't find it, but it was a bright, funny, pixie face, and it warmed before Meredith's look. "So how's your love life?" Jean asked suddenly. It was her standard question.

Meredith turned to the subject gratefully. "Same. Still Barry."

"Things getting serious there, are they? You guys have

52

been going together now, what, six, eight months?"

Meredith offered her fingers to a lamb nose. "Yeah, about. I don't know about serious, though. I think he is. He says he loves me. Then he gets all bent out of shape when I don't say it back."

Jean stretched out on the grass on her stomach and pulled a dandelion stem from its mooring, carefully, so that the white crown of fluff stayed intact. "Loaded words, Merry. Those are loaded words, because they mean different things to different people, and it's hard to know how someone is going to take them. I feel love for you because you're a neat person and I can see lots of good qualities in you, including some of your dad's good qualities that I love in him. Which is not the same kind of I-love-you that I mean when I say it to Robert, or to my animals or God or"—she waved her hand in a broad arc and sent fluff-borne dandelion seeds parachuting through the air—"the world in general."

"I know that," Meredith said impatiently. "That's how I feel, too, especially about Barry. Sometimes I just want to hold him and, I don't know, mother him maybe, and that gives me this big rush of loving feeling toward him, but then other times I want to be mothered myself. Well, I don't mean mothered exactly."

"Nurtured," Jean said.

"Yeah. Like that. Something like that. And Barry just doesn't seem, I don't know, big enough. Substantial enough. Well, you met him that time, you know. Maybe it's just physical size. We're exactly the same height, I'm even a little heavier than he is. I wonder if I'd feel differently about him if he was six inches taller than me."

Jean made a warm laughing sound and propped her chin on her crossed wrists. "Oh, I expect it's more than that. I think you're the stronger one in more important ways than physical size, and probably that holds you back."

Meredith pondered. "He has this, I don't know, this sort of fragile-ness about him. I could hurt him so easily, and I don't want to." She pounded the ground with her fist. "Sometimes when I think about my mom and dad, how much damage they did to each other just by loving each other, whew, it really scares me."

"It wasn't the loving that did the hurting."

Meredith looked at her.

"It wasn't loving each other that hurt them," Jean repeated more strongly. "Well, in a way it was, just because the love was still pulling them together at a time when they each had other needs that were pulling them away from each other. They were both fighting for, well, probably self-preservation, but they still cared very deeply for one another, and that conflict hurt both of them. They both were forced to inflict pain on the person they loved most in the world. It would be like me having to torture Crabby Mary over there, or Zelda or Francis." She waved toward the ewes who lay dozing against the trunks of the apple trees.

"Well, that's what I mean," Meredith argued. "If they didn't love each other there wouldn't be all that pain."

Jean smiled. "Remember that old song, 'The Best Things

in Life Are Free'?" She shook her head. "Wrong. The best things in life cost the most. But you just go ask your dad, or your mom, either one, whether they'd rather have had a life without pain and without each other, and you. See what they say."

Barry flashed through Meredith's mind suddenly, with his leaning toward oblivion rather than pain.

"Come on," Jean said, getting to her feet, "lunch will be gone by the time we get there."

They helped each other over the fence and walked slowly toward the house.

5

After lunch Meredith and Mike drove to Elgin, forty miles away, to relieve Jean's husband at the Farmers' Market stand. The market was held in a grassy meadow just inside the gates of the county fairground. It was a simple market, just a ring of pickup trucks and vans scattered over the grass, with an open area in the middle for buyers to wander through. Display tables beside the rigs held garden produce, antiques, junk parading as antiques, craft items, and even exotic poultry and rabbits.

Meredith had been there on other Saturday afternoons, but none with weather as perfect as today. It's like God is teasing us, she thought, giving us a day like this when it might be the last. Or maybe not teasing, maybe . . . rewarding. Maybe one final gift. One perfect day.

Panic thickened her throat. Last day, last day. I'm wasting it. I should be . . . I don't know . . . cramming everything into today, and all I'm doing is ordinary stuff.

She got out of the pickup and followed Mike through the

long trampled grass toward the familiar blue and white panel truck with its refrigerated cargo area for keeping the produce fresh from farm to buyers' hands. A blue and white striped awning canted out along one side of the truck, and in its shade was a low display table, a couple of lawn chairs, and Robert Ling. He raised his hand in greeting, but glanced away only briefly from a tiny television set on the ground beside him.

"Anything new?" Meredith asked.

Robert shrugged. He was tall and narrow, with stooped shoulders and a small pot belly and a forward-jutting head that seemed too heavy for his neck. His face was round, flat-featured, with an Oriental agelessness and a soft-lipped sweetness that Meredith loved. He had come to Chicago from Singapore, earned a doctorate in electrical engineering, and married a woman who made a career out of profitable alimony settlements. She left Robert after seven months of marriage, with an ironclad grip on half of his sizable salary, for life. He quit his job, married Jean, who was living on the farm then, and happily settled into a life that produced almost no dividable cash income.

Meredith went around behind his chair where she could see the television screen and draped her arms around Robert's neck. He ran his hand up and down her forearm in quick, nervous motions. "How you doing, Merry?"

"About the same as everyone else, I guess," she said. "Scared out of my gourd. How you doing?"

He shrugged under her arms. She rested her chin on the

57

top of his head and smelled the softly musty smell of his coarse hair. Suddenly she loved Robert and her father and this fairground and everyone in it. She had an eye-stinging urge to embrace the earth and hold on tight.

Mike said, "Boy, you could shoot a cannon through this crowd and not hit anybody. Did you do much business at all this morning?"

"Very little." Robert's words vibrated up through Meredith's jawbone and skull, making her want to giggle. "I guess everybody want to stay home today and watch the news. I sold maybe forty, fifty dollar worth of stuff. Funny thing, Mike. The flowers went right away. Even the lilacs, and you know how slow they usually sell. People seem like they want something pretty to look at today, not something good to eat. Go figure it."

Meredith walked with Robert toward where the pickup was parked. "Robert, have you got any ancient Oriental wisdom for an occasion like this? I mean like, did Confucius say anything that would come in handy here?"

"Confucius say, 'Man who lie down with dogs get up with fleas.' "

"What's that got to do with anything?"

Robert shrugged and laughed. "That was the only Confucius I could think of on short notice. But I got a good pig joke for you. You want to hear a good pig joke? This traveling salesman called on a farmer, see, and he's looking at the farmer's pigs. He sees one pig got a wooden leg, so he say, 'How come your pig got a wooden leg?' Farmer say, 'That one is a very special pig. She our pet. She save my family's life when our house catch on fire and she squeal and wake us all up. That one very special pig.' So the salesman he say, 'Yes, but why she have that wooden leg?' and the farmer say, 'Listen, buddy, a pig *that* special, you don't eat her all at once.' "

Robert threw his head back and laughed, and Meredith laughed with him. Her laugher was tight and metallic at first, but it loosened her inside, gathered momentum until the tears spurted. She stopped walking and leaned into Robert and cried.

"I don't want to die, Robert. Can't you do something? Can't anybody *do* something to stop this?"

But Robert couldn't help her. He was crying, too, as he held her and rocked her.

"I got to go home," he said finally. "Don't tell anybody you saw me cry, okay? I got a reputation as a cold Oriental to uphold."

Meredith sniffed. "I won't tell if you won't. I love you, Robert. I just wanted you to know that, in case . . ."

He waved off her words and climbed into the truck. "It's not going to happen. I'll see you, maybe next weekend, okay? The shearer is coming next weekend to do the ewes. Jean would be glad for your help cleaning the fleeces. Okay?"

Meredith nodded. She knew what he was doing, the same thing her mother used to do when Meredith was small and frightened of a doctor's appointment. Focus on something beyond the scary moment. A trip to the Brookfield Zoo after the shots at the doctor's office. Think about next weekend to get past this one.

She smiled and waved him off.

On the far side of the fairgrounds were a cluster of long barns including one in which town residents kept their horses. From that direction three riders approached. Meredith stood in the sun watching them. They were all young, younger than she. She wanted to wave to them, to stop them and tell them that she had never been on a horse in her life, only the iron deer in the lilac park. She wanted to ask them to share with her, now, while there was still time.

But they rode by and she didn't ask. She ached for all of the lives she would never live, even if this life went on. She would never be a child growing up on a ranch in the west, with her own cow pony, solving mysteries about rustlers and abandoned gold mines.

She would never be the child of sophisticates, growing up in an elegant Manhattan townhouse and spending her Saturdays in art museums, nor a solitary child on a remote cattle station in the Australian outback, getting her schooling over a two-way radio and having miniature kangaroos for pets.

There was only her one life, and maybe not even that, and *it wasn't enough*.

She went back and sat in the lawn chair beside her father and put her feet up against the display table with his. Only a few shoppers wandered through the market, and none came close.

"Dad, what do you think God is, anyway?"

60

Mike looked at her. "You don't ask any easy ones, do you? What do I think God is? I never really decided, Mare. Possibly an invention of men, a long time ago, because they needed explanations for creation and the universe and all the unexplainable things that happen. Maybe it's a basic human need, to believe there's something more powerful than us, to pull our fat out of the fire when things get out of control. You know, go to church every Sunday and say your prayers, and nothing bad will happen to you. Or if terrible things do happen, you can say, God is testing me. I'll have a better life in heaven because I've had it so hard here on earth."

"You don't believe that?"

He shrugged. "I don't happen to believe that there is one supreme bearded old-man-type God who takes roll on Sunday mornings and keeps track of individual lives. I certainly don't believe there's a God who kills babies to punish sinning parents, or anything like that. I think religion in the early centuries was a tool in the hands of the ruling class. Back then there were a very few rich and powerful men, and hordes of very poor and powerless people. What better way to keep the poor under control, and enslaved, than to threaten them with hell?"

Meredith pondered. "Does that mean you're not a Christian?"

"Look, you asked for my opinion on this subject and I'm giving it to you because we never really have talked about it and it's important. But remember, this is just my personal opinion. Yours is up to you to find, okay? No, I'm probably not actually a Christian. To me all religions are very much alike in the basics, and they are good or bad in direct proportion to whether they produce good or bad people, that is, people who treat one another with compassion or cruelty."

"So then, do you think there is no such thing as God? Or life after death?" Her voice weakened.

He reached for her hand and swung it between their chairs. "I didn't say that. There may very well be a God, maybe in the form of a universal consciousness, some vast unimaginable mass of life force that all of us individuals are split off from while we go through this life, and then join again later. Or maybe we evolve into some higher life form after this existence, like we do when we go from being unborn babies in a womb out into this life. Maybe we were created by any number of higher-ups. I just don't know, and I won't know until after I go through the death experience for myself, and the truth of the matter is that no one else really knows, either, including the religious folk who claim revelations."

"But you do think we exist some way, after . . ."

"Yes, I do. I don't know it for a fact, but it seems logical to me. It seems in keeping with the cyclical nature of . . . nature. A leaf falls from a tree, rots into the ground, is absorbed back into the tree's system as nourishment, and eventually some of those molecules are back there at the end of that branch, as another leaf. Not the same leaf, mind you, but . . . nothing is ever completely lost in nature, and I can't imagine that something as powerful as a human soul could vanish."

A woman with three small children orbiting around her stopped in front of them and bought ten pounds of snow peas. As Mike handed her the change he said automatically, "Thank you now. You have a nice day."

She gave him a hollow-eyed look and walked away.

They sat silently for a long time, holdings hands.

Meredith said, "Do you think a nuclear war would be the end of the human race, then?"

Slowly Mike nodded.

"But you said you didn't think human souls could be destroyed."

"Souls, no; bodies, yes. Sure. When you take the long view of it, *Homo sapiens* is just one species out of the millions of life forms on this planet. Right now we happen to be the ruling animal. It hasn't always been us; why should we think it will always be us?"

"Really?" Meredith stared at him.

"Sure. It used to be dinosaurs. Heck, sixty-five million years ago this whole place was dinosaur-land, and the little guys that were our ancestors were like, say, rabbits are to us. An insignificant link in the biological chain."

"So what happened?"

"Well, what we think happened was something like an asteroid shower that created a dust cloud over the earth."

"Like a nuclear winter would be?"

"Yes, on that order. It changed the environment so much that the dinosaurs died out. Our little ancestors survived and gradually took over. But never forget, honey, they could never have taken over and developed into what we are today if the dinosaurs hadn't been gotten out of our way by that asteroid shower or whatever it was. We could never have competed with them otherwise."

Meredith absorbed that for a long quiet time.

She said, "Last night on that television special they were saying that probably the only life form that could survive a nuclear winter would be the insects. Does that mean that, if it happens, and human beings are . . . wiped out . . . that some kind of insect is going to start evolving into super-insect and take over the universe?"

"Not the universe necessarily, but this planet, sure, it could happen."

"But that's crazy. That's like some science fiction movie."

"So are a lot of other things we're living with every day and accepting as normal."

Meredith shuddered. "Oh, awful. Insects running the earth."

"Not awful for them," Mike said mildly. "Sure, it sounds terrible for us because we belong to the species that might be on its way out. The dinosaurs probably said the same thing about the hairy little mammals they were munching up for breakfast. Who's to say that some future form of insect might not do a better job of husbanding this planet than *Homo sapiens* has been doing this past sixty-five million

64

years? Maybe it's time to give somebody else a turn at the wheel."

Although she didn't understand why, Meredith found an odd sort of comfort in Mike's ideas. They seemed to take her back a giant step from the emotional center of the situation so that she could glimpse a time span of millions of years backward and forward, with the earth surviving even the very worst, a nuclear holocaust and its winter aftermath, and becoming green and live again. A line of poetry came into her mind.

> "And there beneath the winter's snow, the grass
> of next year's spring, already green."

It made her own lifespan almost invisibly insignificant, so that it was of no great importance whether it lasted sixty more years or sixty more hours. Important to her, yes, in the loss of myriad pleasures, but no more than that.

Again she was aware of tingling sensations throughout her body, brightened colors and clarified distant voices of the children returning on their horses. She felt a need to run and jump in the air, to sweat and gasp for breath and push herself to untested limits.

She got up. "I'll be right back. I have to go ride a horse."

Three o'clock. Four o'clock. As the afternoon slipped past, Meredith found herself more and more often looking at her watch. Three hours till the deadline. Two and a half hours . . .

She and Mike packed away the unsold peas and asparagus,

rolled up the awning, and folded away the chairs. She un-
plugged the television from the cigarette lighter in the truck's
cab and settled it on the floor between her feet. There was
an unspoken assumption between them that Mike would
drive her home.

"What time will we get there, do you think?"

He glanced at his watch. "Six-fifteen, six-thirty. I don't
think there'll be much traffic this evening. Do you want
to stop somewhere for supper? There's a Kentucky Fried
Chicken place up here on the highway. We could get a
bucket of extra crispy if you want, and eat while we drive."

Meredith thought. "I don't think I could eat anything. You
get some if you want."

But they drove past the airborne striped bucket. Traffic
on Highway 59 was unusually light. They circled up onto
the expressway just as the blue vapor lights were coming on
to illuminate the cloverleaf. From the radio came muted
reports: the President and UN spokesmen repeating requests
for peaceful negotiations with Verdura's governor.

The truck bored east into the darkening blue of the evening sky. The Dippers were clearly visible above the trees,
and Orion and the North Star. Meredith leaned forward
toward the windshield to see them.

"If it happens," she said, "When do you think, I mean, how
soon would they, would the rockets . . ."

Suddenly a light flashed across the sky, arcing downward
toward the city before them.

Meredith screamed.

66

The truck swerved onto the shoulder and bounced to a halt. Mike threw his arms across Meredith, around her head, pulling it down into his chest.

"Oh Jesus, oh God, here it comes," he breathed.

Silence.

Slowly they sat upright and looked out. Blue-black night and blue-white lights from houses and headlights. Their world, untouched.

Seconds ticked past.

"It wasn't anything," Meredith said finally, her voice weak.

"Shooting star, must have been." Mike let his breath out. "Whew, I thought we'd bought it for sure."

Laughter trembled from both of them, and Mike had trouble steadying his hand to turn the ignition key.

Back on the expressway and approaching the Lombard exit, Meredith said, "Dad? Just one thing I want to get on the record, okay? If . . . it happens . . . I'm glad I was with you today, and I'm glad we're all going to be together tonight. Not that you and Mom can do anything, I realize, but I'm glad we're going to be together."

"Me too, darling daughter." His voice was thick through the words.

6

Saturday morning, as the sky gradually lightened beyond his bedroom windows, Barry lay sprawled in the middle of his bed, as awake as he had been through most of the night. There had been only one lapse in his awareness, around three o'clock, and that had left him with vague sickening traces of a dream he didn't want to remember.

The dread that twanged him into alertness was the same kind he felt before any expected physical pain. A dental appointment when he knew from tongue probing that he had cavities gave him this same sick longing to escape the inescapable. He felt the novocaine needle a hundred times, imagined it piercing his gums, and shuddered. No amount of earphone music protected him from the whine of the drill.

He had grown up balanced between anguish and gratitude at his maleness. The anguish was for expectations: riding on ski lifts, driving on expressways, and the big one, being drafted and forced into combat duty. The gratitude was for the escape from pregnancy. He honestly believed he would go insane if there were another human being growing inside him, inevitably, inescapably ripping him apart to gain its own life.

He'd been spared that only to face, at last, the ultimate fear. It had been in the background of his life always, but it had been too big to comprehend. The ant never saw the human being who stepped on it, only a shadow and possibly in that last instant a small portion of shoe sole. Never the whole threat.

Now, like an unborn child to a pregnant woman, the nuclear threat could no longer be ignored. As clearly as he saw the room around him Barry could see his world burned out, bombed out, ashed over, the poison everywhere, dead and rotting bodies underfoot, and the gray cloud of nuclear winter spreading its haze around the planet.

Last night's dream came flashing into his mind; looking down at his hand he had seen flesh rotting away from the skeleton; still alive. Alive but in agony. No.

No.

Alive and somehow prevented from ending his life. That was the real fear; pain beyond bearing and no way to end it.

Barry's face was damp with sweat, but a clammy chill made him thrash his way deeper into the blanket as he twisted onto his side, knees up.

He decided not to get up. Not ever. Just lie there until he painlessly passed out of his body and into floating invisibility. Untouchability. Yes. That was the way out.

"Barry," Joel bellowed from downstairs, "stir your stumps.

I've got to leave by ten. Get on down here. I'll be out on the court."

Barry groaned and swore into his pillow, but finally he groped for his glasses and rolled out of the bed.

After Dad leaves I'll come back to bed and stay there till the world either blows up or doesn't. Tonight. Eight o'clock eastern, seven central. God, even the end of the world comes out sounding like a TV special. It is, though, isn't it? We all sit around watching the news bulletins on the tube and then for the grand finale . . .

As a small rebellion against his father's insistence on normality this morning, Barry left his toothbrush untouched. So his mouth tasted gummy, so what? Big deal. Decay-causing plaque could just build up in there to its heart's content, he didn't give a damn.

He came downstairs on heavy heels, ignoring his mother's cheerful good morning from the living room, ignoring the inappropriate hunger twinges in his stomach, and slammed out through the kitchen door.

It was a beautiful morning. There was no way he could get around that. His heart squeezed at the sight of the sky, the rich dark green of the hedge along the driveway, and the silver shine of his little Civic. God, how he loved that car. Only five months old, if you counted a car's birthday from the day you bought it. Eighteen hundred thirty-two miles on it. Traces of the glue from the window sticker still showed on the glass; he'd been careful not to wash it off. He wanted everybody to know it was a new car.

He loved the Civic not for its intricacies under the hood, as some of his friends loved their cars, but for the marvel of mobility and escape it gave him. When things got unbearable at home, his little silver bullet bore him over to Meredith's or wherever he wanted to go.

This morning, as he stood against the car, his hand on the sun-warmed hood, he saw the car as his partner in another kind of escape. The permanent one. Close your eyes and aim into a tree or off a cliff. One big collision and he'd be free, floating above the wreckage, watching the ambulance and the patrolmen and the gathering crowd. Watching his parents cling to each other, weeping and loving him. Finally loving him.

"Barry, come on, I haven't got all day." Joel appeared on the path beside the garage swinging two tennis rackets, his pockets bulging with lime green balls and an irritated expression on his face.

"Here goes family hour," Barry muttered.

At the edge of the court they paused to divide the balls, but Barry's jeans were too tight to admit more than one ball in each pocket and that was a stretch.

Joel said, "Here, I want you to try the aluminum racket this time. See if you don't like it better. Here, heft it once, get a feel of the balance."

"Did you watch the news this morning, Dad? What's the situation?"

"Same. Nothing new overnight. You take the far court first."

71

"Dad, does this strike you as just a little bit stupid?"

"Stupid, what? What does?"

"This." Barry's voice rose. "You and me standing out here talking about aluminum tennis rackets as though they were *important*, for God's sake. What if it happens, tonight, like they're talking about? What if it really does happen, Dad? If this turns out to be our last day . . ."

"What?" Joel attacked. "What should we be doing, Barry? Praying?"

"Yeah, maybe. I don't know. Who knows?" He waved his arms helplessly. "I just feel like we ought to be using this time for something more important than a tennis lesson, is all."

Joel marched away toward his serve corner and waved Barry toward the far court. "Get over there."

Barry trotted past the net and took up his position, knees flexed, left hand cradling the racket, bouncing it, ready for his father's first gunshot serve. The funny thing was, he knew that a part of himself was on the verge of enjoying this moment. It was Saturday, the air was cool-warm and fragrant with spring smells, the aluminum racket felt light and ready in his hand, and the challenge of conquering his father's serves raised a kind of hard joy in him. He thought, All I have to concentrate on right now is that little green ball over there in his hand. Nothing else has to be thought about.

But when the ball came to him it came too fast, too short. It came at his left side and there wasn't time to get around it. He swung backhand, already knowing his balance was off.

The ball struck the rim of the racket and bobbled to the ground.

"Leave it," Joel shouted. "Now this time be ready. I'll give you another one just like that one, and I want you to be *ready* this time. Throw your weight behind it. If you have to miss, miss it as hard as you can, but don't hold back. That's your trouble, you hold back."

Barry clenched his jaw and delivered a hard backhand swathe; the ball bounced past untouched.

"Heads up," Joel yelled.

This time Barry swung and connected but the racket was angled awkwardly. Net ball.

"You're not concentrating," Joel bellowed. "Get with the program here."

"*You* get with the program," Barry snarled. The ball hit him in the chest as he walked toward the net, his racket dangling forgotten from his hand. At the net he stopped and stood there, leaning slightly into the canvas binding at the top of the net because he had to lean against something or someone.

"Don't hang on that thing. Get back there. Let's work on your serve. Barry?"

"Let's not work on my serve, Dad." His voice was soft.

Joel came up and said, with overdone patience, "All right, what's your trouble?"

Airily Barry said, "Oh, not much, Dad. Just the usual, you know, there's a nuclear bomb aimed at me with some maniac getting ready to push the launch button, the whole world is on the edge of being blown to hell, this may be the last day of our lives, I can't seem to get enough power into my backhand, you know, Dad. Just the usual."

For a long moment they stood staring at each other, eyes level, the challenge in Barry's gradually melting to appeal; the anger in Joel's growing stronger. Then Joel dropped his racket and turned and walked away.

Barry ran after him, dodging around the end of the net. "Dad. Wait. I need you."

He grabbed his father's arm and spun him around and said again, "I need you. I can't handle this alone. Tell me what to do, Daddy."

Joel's face was set and distant and drained of color. He shook his head.

Barry wrapped his arms around his father, but Joel's arms went on hanging lifeless at his sides.

"I can't tell you anything," Joel whispered. "I can't make it go away. There's nobody to help *me*. . . ."

Slowly Barry let go and stepped back. "Did you *ever* love me? I know you don't now. I never do anything right, so how could you? But did you ever? Dad? When I was a little baby, did you hold me, or didn't you want to?"

Joel's voice was a strained semi-whisper. "I held you. I wasn't very good at it, but I held you. Yes. You were our miracle, did you know that? Did you know your mother had five miscarriages before you were born? And that she had to stay in bed for six months with toxemia while she carried you?"

"You really wanted me, then?"

"Yes. A son, a man's son, that's like starting his own life all over again. Getting things he didn't have, accomplishing things he never could. Going on from where he leaves off, you know."

"Going into his law firm?"

"Yes, that's part of it, sure."

"But did you want *me*?" His voice broke with passion.

"I just said so."

"No. You said you wanted another *you*. You didn't say you wanted me, me, Barry, the separate person. Hell, I'm not about to carry on past where you got to. I'm not as smart as you, I won't be as good a lawyer as you, I'm never going to have any kind of damn backhand. What's the point of having me? Huh? What's the point? You can do it all better yourself. Why not just *do* it yourself and get off my back?"

"What are you mad about? I don't understand what you want from me, Barry."

"No, you don't, do you? You never did, you never will."

"What? Tell me," Joel yelled.

"I can't," Barry shouted back. "You have to *know* without me spelling it out for you."

"You want too much from me!"

"I just want you to love me."

Joel's voice dropped again. "I'm trying, son."

They stood silent, while tears rose in Barry's throat and threatened his eyes. Then abruptly Joel shrugged, waved his hands helplessly, and turned and walked away.

For a long electric moment Barry looked after him. Then he threw his racket away and ran to his car. Meredith. He needed Meredith.

At the Algonquin, nobody answered his ring on the 6B buzzer. He drove out St. Charles Road to the clinic. At the reception desk Janice halted him. "Dr. McCoy is with a client. Anything I can do?"

"You don't know where Meredith is this morning, do you?"

"I believe she went out to see her dad."

Barry slammed out and sat hunched in his car, fuming with frustration. With her father. Inaccessible, when he needed her most. And with her father.

His mind began to replay the scene with his own father, substituting Mike McCoy for Joel Franklin. The words would have been different. The hug would have been returned. The hug would have been offered as soon as Barry's need for it showed in his face. The humiliation of asking for it would have been avoided. And somehow Mike McCoy would have come up with words that would have helped.

Savagely he threw the car into gear and spun into the traffic with a shower of gravel rising in his wake. He headed west, toward Meredith and her father, then realized he didn't know the way to the farm. He'd only been there once, and Lee had driven that day. Besides, he might not be welcome. Mare might prefer to have her father to herself today.

That thought made his stomach rancid.

When he came to Highway 64 he turned east instead of west, east toward the Eisenhower Expressway and downtown. There was no clear reason in his mind, just an urge that he didn't even want to dissect.

At the expressway's entrance ramp he gunned the car forward, blanking from his mind the knowledge that this would be his first time on the expressway, where the speed limit was a joke and driving slowly was as dangerous as keeping up with the flow. He merged with the traffic around him. For a suspended moment there was dizziness in his head and a numbness in his arms and hands. He pictured the car attaching to an invisible conveyor belt and being pulled along with no effort on his part.

But then the Civic swerved lightly to the right; he over-corrected and came within screaming distance of a semi on his left. The wind from the truck blew the little car back into its own lane.

Fear sweat prickled on Barry's face and the backs of his hands. He gripped the wheel and hunched forward, elbows out, eyes staring at the car ahead in his lane. Everything else disappeared from view. Just that car, that lane. He eased into a slightly slower speed and instantly the space in front of the Civic was filled with another car that floated in from the side.

With a feeling of mounting panic Barry tried to move his head and eyes to the right long enough to watch for an opening in that stream of traffic so that he could begin to work toward an exit, but when his head moved right, the Civic drifted right, too.

I could just close my eyes and let go, he thought. The

car will crash into something, I'll get thrown around for maybe thirty seconds, a minute tops, and then it will be all over.

But that would wreck the gleaming silver metal of the Civic. And it might kill other people, too, and probably most of them wouldn't want to die.

Some of them would deserve it, though. Maybe all of them. All of us. Maybe it really is time to erase human beings and start over again.

At the sides of his vision Barry was aware of rows of ugly brick apartment buildings closing in around the expressway. Ugly buildings full of people who were poor, sick, hopelessly trapped. All his life he'd passed these buildings and felt a sort of contempt for people who allowed themselves to be stuck in that life. Why didn't they escape? Why did they have to live with weedy pavement and broken glass and gobs of spit on the sidewalks, and the smells!

Now he thought, if it happens, those people are going to be glad to get out of their lives. Through his mind flashed pictures of his own world, full of room and fragrant air, and clean spaces and surfaces everywhere he looked. He had everything these poor people around here couldn't have, and it still wasn't enough, so just think how miserable their cruddy lives must make them.

Unless. Unless those people loved each other enough to make up for where they had to live. Like all those stories about poor but happy families . . .

"Damn him. Would it have killed him to put his arms around me just once?"

Suddenly Barry realized that his lane and the one to his right were peeling away from the expressway, curving away into the air in a downward spiral. He touched the brakes to slow for the curve. There it was in front of him. The way out. Just let the car go straight. Just sail out into the air . . . Yes. Now!

But his hands betrayed him. They bore down on the wheel and eased it to the right, and with only a brief wobble to mark his decision, the instant passed and the Civic coasted down onto Halstead Street.

7

Barry left his car in a parking lot on Washington and began to walk. There was an urge in him to find the worst and the ugliest of humanity, to immerse himself in lives that would be no great loss to the universe. He didn't think he could stand looking at anything else today.

He turned corners at random, going from warehouse blocks to tenements to open areas where razed buildings had not yet been replaced. The city air was acrid, so that he didn't want to touch his lips with his tongue for fear of tasting it. The stores he passed had iron mesh gates to protect their windows, rolled back now in the daylight hours but still visible.

The people on the sidewalks were a mixture of black, white, Chicano, Oriental. He avoided looking directly into their faces as they passed, but he was aware of them in a way he had never been aware of strangers before. These are actually poor people, he told himself, and he tried to see a common denominator in them, a way of carrying themselves, perhaps, that would label them "poor." Some shuffled and hunched over and seemed beaten down by their lives, but others moved with determination or distraction or anger; the children were just children, and ran.

Barry felt uncomfortable among them. His jeans and polo shirt seemed too bright and smooth and clean. He felt obvious; the rich kid coming among them to stare. But that was stupid, of course. No one could know why he was there. He didn't know himself, so how could they?

In the doorway of an empty store an old man lay curled up and smiling, his head pillowed on an old sweater, his foot lolling out into the sidewalk traffic. His pants were unzipped. Barry hesitated, wanting to lean over and zip him up, but he was afraid to. He turned and walked on.

Gradually he began looking more closely at the faces that passed him. As far as he could tell no one was worrying about the bomb. The faces were as blank as he guessed they usually were. He thought about stopping people and asking them what they thought about the Verdura crisis, pretending to be a reporter doing man-in-the-street interviews. But he had no notebook, no clipboard and cameraman. No one would take him seriously.

As he approached a parked car with several teenage boys leaning against it, sitting on it and in it, Barry tensed. They looked at him. He fastened his eyes on something up the block and kept walking.

"Hey, you lookin' for something?" one of them called out. Barry ignored him.

They laughed among themselves. Another voice called, "Hey, you lookin' for some action? You need you a little female companionship? I can fix you up, any color you want, okay?"

Barry was past them now, but they left the car and fell in behind him. He walked faster. "No thanks," he called.

One small boy eased up beside Barry and said, "You shopping? I got it all: speed, acid. If I ain't got it I can get it. Best prices on the street, and it's premium goods. Guaranteed."

"No thanks." Barry's voice was tight; fear prickled his scalp. He walked faster.

Behind him the voices laughed but they fell away. Openly shaken now, Barry turned at the next corner and headed back toward Washington Boulevard and his car. Washington should have been the next street, but the sign said "Union." He paused, confused. South was this way, wasn't it? Or . . . no . . .

He turned and began walking again, looking for someone to ask. The direction felt wrong. He turned again and walked several blocks, straining to see each new street sign as it came into view. Avoiding the street where the gang had followed him, he went on, growing increasingly uneasy in this hostile place.

Passing a shoulder-high remnant of wall from a demolished building, Barry saw the top of a very small tree in the space beyond the wall. He slowed and looked in, hungry for the sight of something as reassuringly Lombard-y as a tree.

Then he stopped completely and leaned his arms on the cinderblock top of the broken wall.

It was a kind of garden, no more than twenty feet square, walled on two sides by raw buildings whose flanks still showed remnants of stairways and wallpaper and paint. They had been rooms, homes. On the third side of the little park was the wall where Barry stood, and the fourth side opened on to an alley.

Most of the area was covered with rubble, chunks of brick imbedded in concrete, but in the center was a five-foot square of genuine grass, with a tiny tree growing out of its center. In some places the rubble had been laid flat to form paths, and along one of the walls the chunks of concrete had been wrestled into a low retaining wall that held a flower bed.

There was a woman in the park, working with her back to Barry against the far wall. She was struggling with a large piece of concrete, trying to work it loose from its pile. Barry moved without thinking, around the wall and into the alley.

"Here," he said, "I'll hold this up, see if you can get it out that way." He gripped the rough edge of the piece that lay atop the one the woman was struggling with.

She looked up at him, momentarily startled. Then she grinned and heaved, and her chunk came loose. She was short and thick, and her smile was full of gold teeth. She wore jeans and a wildly flowered smock and combat boots. Her hands were bloody raw.

"You hurt your hands," Barry said.

"Got into a little glass," she puffed. "Ain't nothing serious. Can you grab that end there? I want this one for my corner piece. This way." Grunting, she steered Barry and the concrete chunk to the corner of the two standing walls. They maneuvered it into place against the end of the existing flower bed and wriggled it until it was wedged solidly.

"Whew," the woman said as she wiped her bloodied palms against her thighs and looked at Barry. "I appreciate the help. You got to have a good big solid piece at the corner, to build on, don't you know. I couldn't of done it single-handed."

"This is quite a place." Barry motioned toward the flower bed and the tree. "You didn't build this all yourself, did you?"

"I surely did." She beamed at him.

"Wow." He looked more closely at the hundreds of concrete chunks that had been carefully fitted into paths and retaining wall. The one corner of the area that was still a rubble pile with broken glass and twisted iron reinforcement rods only served to show by its contrast the amount of labor expended on the rest of the space.

There was even a bench of sorts, against the half-wall on the sidewalk side, a bench made of one long rectangular concrete chunk set across a row of smaller ones. "You didn't lift that one by yourself," Barry said, nodding to the bench.

"No, I had some help with that one. My kids give me a

hand with that when they was home at Christmas. They give me that tree, too, five years ago. It wasn't no more than a foot high then, in a plastic pot. It was good company for me, though. I told it, 'You grow for me and stay alive for me, and when you get too big for that pot I'll find you an outside place to grow.'"

Barry looked down into her face. "Is that why you made this place here?"

She shrugged and smiled. "You got to keep your word to a tree. Oh," she laughed, "that was part of it. I just kept walking past this place and looking at it, and whoever owns it kept on not doing anything with it, so I reckoned I would."

"It's nice. It's nice here," Barry said, and he realized he did feel better standing here between the grass and the petunias than he had out on the sidewalk with the chewing gum and spit and drunks. Was it the growing things, he wondered, or this woman, or the sheltered feeling of the place?

"You need some more from that pile?" he asked abruptly.

"Sure, honey. If you got the time I got the rocks." She laughed again and went back to the rubble pile. "What we need now is pieces from about this size up to maybe the size of that one over there. I got to extend this here build-up so the flower bed will go all along this wall, like it does on that one. Watch out for your hands, now. I don't expect you're toughened up to this job. Where you live?"

"Lombard."

85

"Oh. What you doing down here on a Saturday morning?"

"I don't know. I just felt like . . ." He couldn't think how to end the sentence.

"Slumming?"

"Yeah, maybe, something like that." He laughed, embarrassed.

"Nothin' wrong with a little curiosity about the world, boy. There's lots of places I'd like to get a look at before my number comes up. I don't know that I'd choose a place like this, if I was you"—she laughed again—"but you're you and I'm me."

"What did you mean, before your number comes up? Why did you say that?"

Together they bent and lowered the chunk they were carrying into its place. "Watch your fingers," she said. "I didn't mean anything particular. Just said it. Just meant, before I died I'd like to see some other sights than this here neighborhood, which is about all I seen so far."

"But did you say that because you thought—because you think we might—they might bomb us?"

"It's sure a possibility, boy. I wouldn't put it past them."

"But aren't you scared? I mean, here you are out here working on your park just like it's an ordinary day. You're busting a gut to plant flowers and trees when there's a good chance everything is going to die, maybe right now, tonight. Us, the damn flowers, the damn—" He looked at the little tree and saw it swim in the blur of his tears.

"Hey now." Her voice was as soft as her hand patting his

arm, and suddenly Barry was weeping into her shoulder. "There you go, there now," she crooned, holding him and rocking him.

"This is stupid," he gasped. "I don't even know you."

She laughed and led him to the bench and sat beside him while he took off his glasses and wiped up his face as best he could with the tail of his polo shirt. He was half laughing himself by then. "Boy, I don't know where that came from. Listen, I'm sorry. I sure didn't mean to . . ."

"Perfectly all right. I raised six kids. I been cried on good and plenty in my day." She patted his knee. "My name's Mamie Johnson, just so you won't have to feel like you was crying on a perfect stranger."

"Barry Franklin. Whew. I don't know if that made me feel better or worse. I guess it was just that things have been building up. It's like everything is out of control, you know? My dad keeps on at me about everything, my backhand is for the birds, and my grades are never perfect. They're good, but anything less than an A I have to explain, and my mom is always spaced out on tranquilizers so it's just like she's not there at all. I mean, she makes the meals and does the laundry and all that, but if I try to talk to her she doesn't hear me."

Mamie nodded. "She's got a case of the richies, I expect."

"The what?"

"Too much time on her hands. I seen it in lots of rich women. I used to be a housekeeper, different ladies down on Lakeshore. They got nothing to do with their time all day, and nothing real to worry about, like how to make it from one dollar bill to the next. So they start spending their time feeling sorry for themselves, going to psychiatrists and that nonsense. First thing you know they got themselves convinced they're unhappy, next thing you know they disappear either down a bottle or into a medicine cabinet. You give those ladies something real to worry about, like a couple of retarded children to look after and a man who can't work and a home that don't have nothing pretty anyplace about it so you have to make it with your own hands, that'll cure 'em. Kill 'em or cure 'em." She laughed.

Barry looked into those warm brown eyes and felt that he could say anything to this woman. "I've been thinking about suicide."

"Why?" She snorted.

He stared, and shrugged. "I don't know. I just get so down sometimes. Sometimes it seems like the best way out."

"Then you're lazy, boy."

"Lazy?" His eyes widened.

"That's what I said. You're looking for the easiest way, not the best way. Like dying was a way to stay in bed all day and not have to go to school and take a test. Ain't that right?"

"I don't know. I never thought about it that way."

But he had, and he knew it, and her perception startled him.

"Well, you ask me, I can't see anything so wrong with your life that you got to talk about ending it. 'Course, that's up to you. If you figure you're so worthless that there's no point in going on with yourself, then that's up to you. You know your value better than I do. Me, though, I wouldn't never consider putting an end to me. Anybody that can take this old ugly rubble heap and make something pretty out of it, that's one worthwhile old lady, wouldn't you say so?"

Barry grinned. "Yeah, you're right there, Mrs. Johnson."

" 'Course, you been brought up rich, you ain't had my advantages."

"How do you figure that?" He made himself more comfortable on the bench, intrigued by the conversation.

Mamie Johnson shrugged. "You know that old saying, 'Whatever doesn't kill me makes me strong.' Well, I been not-killed an awful lot in my years."

"So what you're saying is I'm a spoiled rich kid with no challenges in my life?"

"Different challenges, boy. Harder to see."

"But this nuclear thing. I mean, even if it doesn't happen today or tomorrow, it's still up there hanging over our heads. We still have to live with the possibility, every day of our lives, that we could be wiped out. I know kids at school that figure, why go to college, why try to build any kind of future for themselves?"

Mamie gave him a hard, direct look. "They're pretty dumb then, ain't they?"

"You think so?"

" 'Course I think so. I didn't get this old without picking up some smart along the way. Life ain't over till it's over, and if you throw away what you got, you're a fool. You could wipe yourself out, sure. Or you could spend your life being so scared of losing it that you'd be just as well off if you did lose it. But those are *choices*, boy. You make 'em, you live with them. Or die from them. But they're *your* choices. That's not some fool in some foreign country blowing your life out of your hands, it's this fool right here." Her finger jabbed Barry's chest.

"I know you're right," he muttered, "but still . . ."

"But still," she whined, taunting him. "Well, you may be a rich kid with nothing better to do than sit around feeling sorry for yourself. Me, I got a flower bed to build. My grandson's bringing me a load of dirt and horse manure this afternoon, he works out at Arlington at the race track, and I got to get this retaining wall finished before he gets here. You want to sit there crying in your shirttail, or you want to give me a hand, which?"

They got up and went back to the rubble pile.

"You are some kind of great old girl, Mrs. Johnson."

"I know that."

Barry stayed until the wall was done, the manure and dirt delivered and tamped into place. Then he followed Mamie Johnson's directions to Washington Boulevard and found his car, and with only a few wrong turns he made his way back onto the expressway and headed west. The sun was almost to the treetops when he turned off at the Lombard exit and followed the familiar streets home.

His world seemed changed in some way that he couldn't

identify. Everything looked bigger, brighter, dearer. With a tightening chest he realized that he did not want to lose this, not any of this. Not himself. Not this rich green world or that row of elm trees or that familiar corner with the house that looked like a castle, or the coral tint to the sky behind the roof of the village hall.

Not himself.

He drove more slowly, seeing nothing now except the realization that Mamie Johnson had awakened a hunger in him. He *wanted* his future, for the first time. He wanted to do something that counted, like building a park out of rubble and horse manure and blood from his own hands.

There was pain in the realization. Mamie had said the life choices were his, but she might be wrong. What he did with his future, yes, that was up to him, but whether or not that future would exist, that choice lay with men and forces he couldn't control or even understand.

8

When Meredith and Mike came through the apartment door, Lee was sitting cross-legged on the floor in front of the television, stroking the cat. She came up onto her feet in a lithe twist that shot the cat in an arc to the floor.

"Oh sweetie, I'm so glad you're home. Hi, Mike. Come on in." Lee hugged Meredith long and hard. "I'm so glad you're home."

"What's happening?" Meredith asked. She dropped to her knees, then sank between outcurved heels as Lee returned to her sitting place on the floor. Mike sat in the big brown chair in the shade of the ceiling-high rubber plant. His hands dangled awkwardly between his knees as though he felt he wasn't allowed to put them anywhere.

Lee said, "It's still a stand-off."

Meredith looked at the digital clock on the video cassette under the television. Six fifty-seven. Three minutes till . . . no, that was silly, she told herself. Nothing's going to happen on the stroke of seven.

There was a two-man CBS anchor team on the television screen. It didn't seem to Meredith that they were saying anything new, just filling time, waiting like the rest of the country. They switched to a White House aide on a large screen behind them, and talked with him about the President's current status. The President was with his advisors in the Oval Office where they were in direct telephone communication with the UN negotiators.

The presidential aide on the anchor team's screen was replaced by a spokesman from Civil Defense giving general information about the workings of the radio and television warning systems. Mike sat back in his chair, and Meredith stirred, breathed a little more deeply.

"Anyone want anything to eat or drink?" Lee asked.

They all looked at each other, thought about it, shook their heads.

"Did you have a good lunch?" Lee asked Meredith.

"Yes, nag. Pork chops and spuds and green and yellow veggies and an acre of salad, satisfied?"

"That's my good little girl."

Meredith made a face.

To Mike, Lee said, "So how are things at Sunnybrook Farm?"

"Don't start with me, okay?" Mike said tensely.

"I'm not starting with you. I'm interested in your life. How are things on the farm? There, was that better?"

Meredith said, "Hey, come on, you guys."

After a pause Mike said, "Things are fine, thanks. Jean's sheep are beginning to lamb. Seven so far, two black ones."

"Good. She wanted black, didn't she? Would you tell her I'd love to get enough of that black wool to make a sweater if she has it to spare, okay? It's such beautiful stuff."

"I'll tell her."

Another pause.

"Have you started selling at your farmers' markets yet?" Lee asked, her voice tightening slightly.

Meredith answered. "We did that today, at Elgin. Me and Dad and Robert."

Lee nodded. "So, you're making out okay then, money-wise?"

"Sure. It doesn't take a forty-thousand dollar income to have a good life, at least not out there."

"Come on, you guys," Meredith pleaded.

Stiffly Mike said, "Look, if you want me to leave just say so. If I'm intruding on you girls' cozy little group here, I can leave."

"Oh Mike, grow up."

"Don't leave, Dad."

Lee glanced at the television screen, then down at her lap. "No, stay. I want you to stay. I need . . ."

Meredith, looking swiftly at her father, saw a flicker of hope cross his face. He didn't move, didn't speak; Meredith sensed that he was afraid to for fear of breaking something in the air. Silently the three of them turned to the television.

Governor Cassals was in front of a battery of TV cameras, speaking in Spanish. A young man standing beside him translated a beat behind the rapid-fire words of the Governor. He was talking about U.S. planes violating Verduran air space.

"That's crazy," Meredith flared. "Who wants their stupid air space anyhow?"

She asked it of Lee but it was Mike who answered. "Wars always appear to start over some insignificant absurdity. It's the retaliation that makes the thing grow out of all proportion. I walk across your lawn and you don't like it, so you walk across my lawn and trample my flowers, so I walk across your lawn and throw garbage on your porch, so you throw a rock through my window, so I run over your dog, so you shoot me. Makes perfect sense."

Mike got up and went to the bathroom. When he came back he came through the kitchen and opened the refrigerator.

"You are hungry," Lee accused. "Why didn't you say so when I asked? I'll make some sandwiches."

The two of them came back to the living room carrying sandwiches and cans of pop, and this time when Lee sat on the floor, Mike lowered himself beside her and passed around the pop cans.

"Wouldn't you hate to be in the President's shoes right now?" Meredith asked.

"I hate being in any of our shoes." Mike's voice shook with

compressed emotion. "I hate all of this. I'm almost to the point of wishing it would just hurry up and get over with, whichever way."

Lee whispered, "I'm so scared."

On either side of her, her husband and daughter moved closer till knees and shoulders were touching. "Me too," Mike and Meredith said together.

A tremble of laughter went through them.

"At least I'm glad we're here together," Meredith said. "Just think how awful it would be to be alone." She wondered where Barry was, if he was at home with his parents, if he would be coming over sometime during the evening. She wanted him here with her, part of her family.

To her father she said, "They won't really do it, will they? They wouldn't really do this to . . . everyone."

He reached around Lee to stroke his daughter's hair where it lay thick and soft over her shoulders. "I hope not. That's all I can say."

"Well, it makes me furious," Lee said suddenly, in a tinny, harsh voice. Meredith stared at her mother's rigid face. "It just makes me furious. They have no *right*, damn it. What right have those men down there got over my life? What? Tell me that!" She turned to Mike, to Meredith, as though they could answer. "I did not give them the right to take everything away from me. I refuse to give them that right!"

Tears coursed down her face. Mike gripped her shoulders and tried to pull her into a hug, but she sat rigid. Meredith stroked her mother's denim-cased leg.

The cat came toward the sandwiches in a silent crouch, extending his nose and whiskers cautiously, watching the people.

"Get out of there, you rotten cat." Lee pushed him away. Her voice cracked between tears and smile. She closed her eyes and tipped her head back, exhausted, against her husband's arm and said, "There is just so much that I can't stand to lose, here."

Silence.

Mike said, "I know, babe. Me too."

"Meredith's future. I *want* that for her. I want to watch her start to college, and meet the man she's going to marry, and start on her career. I want to be there when she has a baby, Mike."

Meredith wept silently.

Lee went on. "I don't want to lose my little hospital or Janice or my clients. I love them all. And I don't want to lose this apartment. My home. My parents."

"How about me?" Mike said in a low voice.

"And you. I don't want to lose you. Oh no, Mike, you are so much of what I love in this life." She gripped his hand on her shoulder and lay her cheek down atop it. Meredith put her hand on his forearm, too, between his wrist and his rolled-up cuff, where the hairs were red and wiry. She stroked them so that they lay flat against his skin.

"Then why did you push me out of your life?"

"I didn't. You left."

"Because you didn't need me. You had Meredith and your

practice. I was extra baggage in your life. When push came to shove you chose your practice over me. You know you did."

Lee shook her head. "It wasn't that cut and dried and you know it. You were acting like a little boy then, Mikey. You were trying to manipulate me into some sort of proof that I loved you. Like you were saying I had to come and live on that crazy farm with you to prove I loved you, and you never even considered what-all it would cost me. I don't mean the money," she said wearily. "It would have cost me myself, some way."

"I don't understand that."

"No, you never did. I don't understand it very clearly myself, but that's what I felt."

"You want to know what I felt?" His voice was rich with emotion.

Lee twisted to look at him, and Meredith let her hand fall away from his wrist. "Yes, I do. I always did, but you never did make me understand that."

"I felt . . . unnecessary in your life. And I felt like I was turning into a commuter."

Lee laughed. "But you were a commuter."

"I know! That's what I mean. There I was riding the morning train to the office and the five-fifteen back home again to the suburbs to my wife and child, just like every other man on that train. And I was doing a job that had nothing to do with *me*, Michael Martin McCoy. Hell, Lee,

98

all the time I was growing up I thought I was going to be a . . . I don't know. A hero."

A giggle sputtered from Lee.

"Don't laugh. It's true. I was going to be a policeman or a conservation officer or forest ranger or ambulance driver or something like that. I wanted to *matter*. I wanted to save somebody's life sometime, even if it was only a herd of deer or an endangered species of fern. I don't know, sure, it sounds silly now, but I never intended to be an insurance under-writer, and every day that I spent riding that commuter train into that job that any number of other people could have done just as well as me, and riding that five-fifteen back to my little home in the suburbs, every day I did that was one more day subtracted from who and what I was. What I was supposed to be. Finally I felt like it was a matter of saving my own life, to break out of it."

"But going to live on Chuck's farm, Mike? What did that have to do with being a hero?" Lee asked reasonably.

Mike pulled away and leaned back against the brown chair. "I don't know. Nothing much, maybe, but it was a chance, right there in front of me. It seemed like the first step, and it was important to me, and then when you wouldn't come with me, that just killed me, Lee. That was just such clear proof that I hadn't even succeeded at keeping your love, along with all the other things I hadn't succeeded at, and you were the most important part. It was like you were the reason I wanted to make myself the best person I could be. If I didn't have you, then what was the point? See?"

No one spoke, but Lee picked up his hand and held it between both of hers. The cat made another approach, this time snagging the top ham sandwich from the stack.

"Hey," Meredith said, "look out, there it goes."

Lee turned and stared at the cat, who was now crouched over his prize beneath the TV stand. "May as well let him have that one." She reached for a sandwich and so did Mike and Meredith. No one was hungry; the emotions in the room had hardened their stomachs. But with the first bite Meredith's hunger woke, and she finished her triangle of bread and meat down to the last corner of crust.

Slowly the evening passed. The news coverage went on, with anchormen gray-faced from weariness and strain, and an increasing sense of repetition and waiting.

Mike levered himself up into the brown chair. Lee curled into the low spot in one end of the sofa and Meredith stretched out on it, her head in Lee's lap. Full-bellied and smug, the cat sprang onto Meredith's stomach and kneaded himself a bed there.

"This is nice," Meredith muttered around midnight. "I wish the three of us . . ."

Silently eyes met eyes.

After a few minutes Mike said to Lee, "I've been sitting here thinking. You know, the one thing I most don't want to lose is you two. The two people I love. Now that this bomb is on the verge of taking everything, I mean everything, my life, my body, my surroundings and belongings, my future, what it comes down to is that losing you two is what hurts the most. And it's not that bomb that made me lose you. I did that myself. Not some idiot in South America. Me. By choice. Isn't that a nice little bit of human irony?"

Meredith lay still, sensing her mother's stillness, feeling the cessation of the unconscious rubbing of Lee's thumb against her arm.

In a low voice Lee said, "It's not irreversible, you know. Not as long as . . ." She nodded toward the television.

Mike turned his head back toward the television, and so did Lee, but their minds were working. . . .

In spite of herself Meredith faded toward sleep, to be bounced back by her mother's sudden shift beneath her head. Sitting up, Meredith looked at the digital clock. One-twenty.

An anchorman was saying with new alertness, "We have a news bulletin, ladies and gentlemen. We've just . . . Is he ready? Is . . . Yes, the President is coming into the pressroom. We switch you now to Washington."

No attempt had been made to polish the President. His hair was rumpled, his eyes reddened, his tie pulled loose from an unbuttoned collar. But his voice was firm.

"I've just spoken to Special Ambassador Gorsuch, spokesman for the UN negotiating team in Verdura. Governor Cassals has agreed to reopen talks with UN negotiators and both Verdura and the United States will abide by their decision. I believe we have live coverage from . . . are they ready? Yes, here . . ."

Governor Cassals and his interpreter came on to the screen, with several other men grouped around microphones, with milling crowds in the background. Meredith strained to follow what he was saying, but the words sounded meaningless to her.

Mike flung himself back against the chair and threw his arms in the air. "Halleluja."

"Does that mean it's all over?" Meredith asked.

"No, not over," Lee said. "They could still screw it up."

"But at least they're talking instead of bombing," Mike said, looking directly at Lee. "That's the main thing. Where there's negotiation there's hope. Meredith, trade me chairs."

9

"Night now."

"Talk to you in the morning."

"Watch your step on that sidewalk there."

It was two A.M. when the Martins and the Jacobmeyers finally stood and stretched and started down the sidewalk toward their respective houses across from and next door to the Franklins. Barry stood and stretched, too, but he wasn't ready to go upstairs yet. Although his parents and their friends seemed to think the crisis was over just because the UN and the Governor were talking, Barry was still uneasy. He still wanted people around him and his eyes open.

Beverly came back from the front door and began picking up ashtrays. Joel stood in front of the television, looking down at it as though trying to decide whether to turn it off.

"Leave it on awhile, Dad. I want to watch."

"I don't think there'll be anything more to see, just more rehashing."

Barry wanted to keep both of them with him, but he wasn't sure why. Ever since he'd come home from town he'd wanted to talk to his mother, his father. But he didn't know what he wanted to say, and there had been no time. The neighbors dropped in one or two at a time and settled before the television. It was like some sort of macabre Superbowl afternoon, Barry thought. He supposed people wanted to be with friends in a time of crisis, but he resented their intrusion anyway. While he was full of the feelings Mamie Johnson had awakened in him, and while the tension of crisis was in the air, he wanted to *talk*.

"Mom, I went downtown today."

She moved toward the kitchen with full ashtrays balanced on her arms. "Oh? That's nice."

Barry got up and followed her and stood beside her while she emptied the butts into the disposal.

"No, Mom, I mean downtown, not Lombard downtown, I mean the Loop. I drove on the expressway."

She didn't answer, just turned on the faucet and rinsed a huge ceramic ashtray, and slotted it into the dishwasher's rack.

"Mom?"

"What, dear?"

Finally she turned and looked at him. Her eyes were clear of the drug haze they usually wore, clear but haggard and distracted.

"Talk to me, Mom. Tell me what you're thinking and feeling. I need you to talk to me."

Slowly she turned off the water and stood facing the sink, her stomach pressed hard against the rim of the counter. "What I'm thinking and feeling. I don't know. It's been a long time since anyone asked me that. I guess I'm out of the habit."

"Tell me what you were thinking tonight, about, you know, the bomb scare and everything. Were you afraid? Are you still?"

"No, not really. Not afraid. I was glad we had that Chex party mix in the freezer left over from bridge club Wednesday night. That keeps so well in the freezer and it makes such a good snack."

"Mom. Forget the food. Talk to me. Why weren't you scared? How could you not be?"

"Of dying, you mean? Why should that scare me? Why would that be so different from living?"

"What?"

He touched her arm and she turned to him. "Did you drive on the Eisenhower, going downtown? I thought we agreed you'd stay off that until you'd been driving longer."

Barry wanted to yell at her. "What difference does that make, for God's sake? Yes. I drove on the expressway. I didn't kill myself. I could have. I almost did. But I didn't. Would you care? If you don't know the difference between living and dying for yourself, what difference does it make what I do?"

"I don't want you to die," she said earnestly.

"I don't believe we've having this conversation."

"You're the important one, Barry. I produced you, that was what your father wanted me for, and I finally did it." She laughed, and the sound was threaded with hysteria.

"I didn't really want to, did you know that? I kept having miscarriages, and every time I did, I thought to myself, as long as I haven't yet given him what he wants from me, he's still going to keep me around. He'll keep me till I give him his son, and then he'll get rid of me. I could never please him, Barry. I tried and tried, but it was always something. I didn't clean under the cushions on the sofa. One time we were having company and I'd tried so hard to have the apartment perfect for his friends, and right there in front of everybody he pulled off the sofa cushion and showed everybody all the dirt and crumbs and paper scraps down in there, and he said, 'Bev was an art history major.' Like it was something to be ashamed of, like it explained why I was no good at anything."

It occurred to Barry that he had never known his mother had majored in art history, or for that matter hardly anything else about her as an individual separate from himself.

He said, "Is that why you started taking all those tranquilizers, Mom? Because you felt like Daddy was pushing you?"

She shook her head emphatically. "I had to take those. The doctor prescribed them. I was getting too nervous and your father didn't like me that way. He said it made him nervous when I jumped up from the table all the time to get things I forgot."

Barry reached for an ashtray and began to rinse it. He had to lean past his mother but she didn't move. He waved it through the air and set it down into the dishwasher.

"But didn't you ever love me, Mom? Even when I was a baby?"

"Of course I loved you. How can you ask that?" She faced him then, her eyes blazing. "You're the only good thing I've ever done in my life. You're the only part of my life I do love. Don't ever ask that question again."

"But I needed to know. I need to know. Nobody ever tells me that, not even Meredith. I need to know it!"

They were silent. Absentmindedly Beverly began lifting dishes out of the dishwasher and drying them with a terry cloth towel. They hadn't yet been washed.

Barry said, "I wish you and Dad didn't depend on me for so much. Why don't you do something with your own life instead of depending on me to be everything for you? I hate that. It makes me want to . . . run away from it, from the pressure."

"Yes," Beverly said in a soft voice, "I know what you mean."

Barry stared at her.

"Mom, did you know I tried to kill myself one time? When I was little."

She looked at him then, a penetrating look that seemed to focus behind his eyes.

He went on. "Remember that Christmas I wanted a dog so bad, and you said I couldn't have one because they were too much trouble in town? I was going to hang myself in my closet. I got my bathrobe cord around my neck and everything. Got up on my toy chest, you remember that blue stenciled toy chest I had? I got up on that and I stood there for I bet half an hour, just thinking about it."

"Yes, I understand," Beverly breathed.

"You do?"

But she didn't answer, so he went on. "I thought if I jumped off and died, Jesus would catch me in his arms and take me to heaven with him, and it would be like when you look out the plane window, you know, when you're flying just above the clouds, remember when we went to Gramma Mac's that time and the clouds were like this really soft puffy carpet right under the plane, like you could walk on it? I thought heaven would be like that, and I could just run and bounce on those clouds all day, and have a dog, and someone up there would love me so much that I'd never run out of love. Jesus or God or somebody up there was just going to wrap me in so much love, Mom. That was my dream."

"Yes," she whispered.

"And I thought you and Daddy would cry so much, and miss me and love me so much, and I could just laugh down at you from heaven because this big somebody up there would love me more than you did. And I wanted to hurt you."

"Yes," she said again. Her eyes reddened and brimmed over.

108

Suddenly Barry realized: "Have you felt that way, too, sometimes?"

She didn't have to answer. Barry moved into her arms and stood there, holding her until she was holding him, too.

She said, "But we did give you a puppy. We had him reserved for you a month before Christmas."

"I know it. But you know what that made me feel like? It made me feel like I had some kind of power to get what I wanted, but only by dying, or threatening to die, or wanting to die. I know it doesn't make sense now. You guys didn't know what I almost did. But to my mind, back then, that was what it seemed like."

His glasses pressed uncomfortably against his nose as Beverly stroked the back of his head and held him, but he didn't move away from her. He needed this too much.

"Mom, I met this lady today, down in the Loop. This little old gal probably sixty or seventy years old. She's building a park, Mom. All on her own. Just this little square place where they tore down a building, just a junk pile really, but she's been dragging these huge hunks of concrete around and making paths and flowerbeds and a little bit of a lawn with a tree growing out of it."

"*A Tree Grows in Brooklyn*," Beverly murmured.

"What?"

"Nothing. It was an old movie. Go on."

They stood apart then, and absentmindedly Barry began replacing the dirty dishes his mother had removed from the dishwasher.

109

"Anyway, I stopped and helped her for a while and we got to talking and I started telling her things I never told anybody before, except maybe Meredith. I told her I tried to commit suicide, and she said I was lazy and stupid. She said she'd never think of ending herself, because she thought she was something special. And she was. I don't even remember exactly what she said now, but somehow or other she made me feel like it was all up to me."

"What was?"

"I don't know. Living, I guess. Making myself into somebody special enough that I wouldn't want to end me. It was like suddenly realizing I had choices. I don't know, it doesn't sound like much when I try to explain it, but there was just something about that old girl that made me want to be like her. Heck, Mom, she really loved herself."

Beverly sighed and smiled. "Well, honey, maybe that's what you and I need to learn to do, huh? Maybe if we could do that for ourselves it wouldn't matter so much. . . . We wouldn't be so dependent. . . ." Her eyes moved toward the living room.

There was a long silence, then Barry said, "You know what? I don't want to be a tax lawyer. Or any kind of lawyer."

Her eyes met his and across her face came a lively grin that Barry hadn't seen in years. "You know what? I never wanted to be a housewife."

Barry laughed. "What did you want to be?"

"I don't know. I never knew, or I forgot."

"Well, if that Governor and that UN team do good down there . . ."

"You're right. Who knows? The opera ain't over till the fat lady sings."

"Your life isn't over till it's over."

"This is more philosophizing than I've done since my college days."

"We ought to wash ashtrays together more often, Mom."

"Yes. We should."

Barry felt light, floating. He turned to go back to the living room, but his instincts told him that this fragile happiness was not yet strong enough to expose to his father. It could still be broken or soured, and he wanted to hold on to it until it was strong enough within him to live and grow and someday hold him up. Like Mamie's tree.

He glanced at the kitchen clock. It was almost three.

"I need to see Meredith," he said. "I just want to drive over there and see if their lights are on, okay? If they're in bed I won't go in, but I really want . . ."

Beverly nodded and motioned with her eyes toward the back door.

He started toward the door, then came back to give her a quick, hard hug. "You're not such a bad old Mom, you know that?"

She smiled a bleary teary smile and pushed him toward the door.

It was a beautiful night outdoors, crisp and clean-smelling and brightly lit with stars. Barry opened his arms and did a whirling waltz turn on his way to the car, then stopped and stood looking up, and yelled toward the south, "Hang in there, negotiators."

10

Meredith opened the door.

"Hi," Barry said. "I took a chance you guys were still up. Can I come in?"

"Well of course, idiot." She pulled him through the doorway and into a hug. "Are you okay? I've been thinking about you all night. I didn't know if I should call over there. I didn't know what you might be into with your folks or if I might wake somebody up. I'm glad you came."

Mike and Lee, who had been dozing together on the sofa, sat up rumple-haired and greeted Barry. Lee said, "Well, it looks like the worst is over, doesn't it?"

"I sure hope so." Barry kept his arms around Meredith.

"Come on in here," she said, and walked him around the corner into the kitchen. "I think they want to be alone," she whispered. "Could you eat something? I was just thinking about a pizza. We've got some frozen ones, I think. Could you split a pepperoni with me?"

"I could eat a whole one and the box." He motioned with his head toward the living room. "What's with them? What's going on?" he whispered.

She moved away from him and lifted the freezer lid. "Mom? You guys want a pizza? There's only one pepperoni and we've got dibs on that. You can have a Canadian bacon or a, hey, here's a Red Baron supreme, you want that?"

"Yo," Mike yelled.

Barry stuck his head around the corner and said to Mike, "I thought you nature freaks only ate health foods."

"That's right. And there's nothing more healthy and natural than pizza. And I could use another Coke, hon, if you've got it."

Meredith had a sudden urge to dance, but the kitchen was too small. With balletlike motions she slipped the pizzas from their cartons, ripped their plastic envelopes, arranged them on cookie sheets, and swooped them into the oven. Then, with the timer set and twelve minutes to wait, she danced into Barry's hug.

She whispered, "I think they might be negotiating peace terms in there. And I don't mean Ambassador what's-his-face."

Barry lit up. "They might be getting back together, you think?"

Meredith shrugged. "Who knows? Possibly. Even if not— I mean, not to the point of living together—I think something good's going on between them. I think they always loved each other. You know, I was thinking, maybe two peo-

114

ple loving each other is not really the same thing as their being good together in a living situation. The two don't necessarily mean the same thing. You can live perfectly happily with, say, a college roommate, without loving that person, if their habits don't drive you up a wall, and on the other hand you might love somebody really deeply but not be able to live the way they have to live."

"You sure got wise all of a sudden," he teased.

They sat at the table, still close, still holding hands. She said, "I guess there's nothing like spending a night almost getting killed to make a person wise. What's been happening with you? Your folks . . . everything okay over at your place?"

"Yes," he said with gentle wonder. "You know, it is. Well, not everything, that would be too much to hope for, even from a night like this one. But it was kind of neat. Mom and I had sort of a talk. Well, the neighbors were over for most of the evening. They didn't leave till just a little while ago. I kept wanting to come over here and be with you but, I don't know, I felt kind of funny about leaving Mom and Dad. I had this weird feeling that if . . . it had happened and the bomb went off, if I wasn't there with them they'd never forgive me." He laughed. "No, it was more like, they depended on me."

Meredith waited for him to go on, and when he didn't, she prodded. "So what about your mom? How was she?"

"Great. She was great. She wasn't doped up or anything, and we talked, better than we ever have that I can remember."

115

"What? What did she say and what did you say?"

He shrugged. "I don't know. Nothing all that world-shaking. The thing is, Mare, we talked. And hugged. And I felt like . . . she was my friend. You know? Well, you know. You've always had that with your mother, with both of your parents. I never have felt that way with either of mine. I've tried with Dad. I tried to get close to him this morning when we were playing tennis, and," he sighed, "it just didn't connect. You know?"

Meredith rubbed his thumb with hers and warmed him with her eyes.

"I went downtown today. Clear downtown, to the Loop."

"What for?"

"I don't know. I just had this urge. I didn't know why at the time, but when I thought about it later I realized I probably went down there because everything is so ugly there. He shivered. "If the world was about to be blown to hell I didn't want to be looking at anything I'd miss very much. You know?"

Her eyes blurred. Softly she said, "I think you . . . love life a whole lot more than you think."

"Yeah, well, then while I was down there I met this really neat little old woman who was building a park out of concrete rubble, so I stayed and helped her for a while and we got to talking. . . ."

"Building a park out of concrete rubble?"

"Yeah. I'll take you down there sometime. You'd love it.

It's got one tree and a petunia bed. But what I started to say was, she was just such a neat person. She made me feel like on the one hand I was the biggest spoiled brat in the world, and on the other hand that I had the potential—I had the *potential*, Mare—to be as super as she was. It was like she was putting all the responsibility for me making something wonderful out of myself right square in my own hands and at the same time showing me by her own example that I was perfectly capable of doing it. If she could, I could, and if I didn't I had nobody to blame but myself. Is any of this making any sense?"

"It is."

"The thing was, coming home I started realizing how much I did not want to lose all the good stuff, you and my family and my home and myself. And then for a while I hated that woman for making me care about it all just when maybe I'd have to lose it anyway."

The kitchen was still except for the muted voices of the television newsmen and the tick of the stove timer. The aroma of pizza began to flavor the air.

Meredith looked at Barry, a long quizzical look. "I haven't heard you sounding that . . . *up* . . . about anything for a long time. Global crises must agree with you."

He shrugged and grinned. "They can make you think, that's for sure."

She wrapped her arms around him and hugged. "I just love you, Barry Franklin."

He became very still. "What did you say?"

"I said I love you."

"Look," Meredith said, "it's starting to get light." She and Barry sat close together on the balcony, on her old sleeping bag that was spread on the floor and against the railing, to make a nest for them. Just to Barry's right was the wall of the building, the open glass doors into the living room, and the backside of the television set. It still glowed with orange inner lights; the voices of the two anchormen still came to them at intervals, when they turned their attention in that direction.

Meredith's head lay back against Barry's chest and shoulder; she held his hand in both of hers in front of her face. They'd been sitting in that position for almost an hour now and her rump was numb, but she didn't want to move, ever. Their view faced east, and there was an overwhelmingly precious sunrise about to happen.

Within the living room Lee and Mike lay spooned together on the sofa, sometimes dozing, sometimes focusing on the television or calling bulletins to Meredith and Barry. By now all four of them were headachy from lack of sleep. Only the cat, stretched smugly on the crest of Mike's hip, slept.

"Hey," Mike said, "I think we made it through the night, troops. We can all go home and go to bed now."

But no one moved. Barry's arm tightened around Meredith, and her fingers tightened around his. Mike pulled Lee in closer to him and the cat rolled over without waking, to sleep on his back in the secure V between man and sofa cushion.

"I know one thing," Mike said to whomever wanted to listen. "I don't think I'll ever be that scared again. I don't think anything can ever really scare me after this experience."

"After the first death there is no other," Lee quoted, her voice almost lost in Mike's sleeve.

"What's that from?" he asked.

"I don't know. Somebody said it once."

Meredith bent Barry's thumb back and said, "We've got a beautiful new day ahead of us. What shall we do with it?"

"I don't know. Build a park?"

"You're weird, you know that?"

"No I'm not. I'm wonderful."

"Well, yes, that too."

He moved his lips through her hair and whispered, "We could go someplace and make passionate love. Make a baby. You said you wanted to."

She jabbed him with her elbow. "Forget it, turkey. I'm out of the mood now. That was just a passing madness."

"I blew it, didn't I?"

They laughed.

Softly, they sobered together and watched the eastern sky pale from apple green to peach.

Meredith thought, I'll never be any happier in my life than I am at this exact second. Right now. This is it! This was worth it.